"Who are you?" the look in her eyes stopping him short.

Fear. She was afraid—of what? Him? Roman felt cold all over.

What had happened that night she went over that bridge? Why had she been there? He'd never understood that. She'd been on a highway she didn't normally travel, on a trip she'd told no one about, carrying divorce papers he would never have signed.

It had just been one of the many strange, horrible things about her death. But...

But Leah wasn't dead.

Dear Reader,

We keep raising the bar here at Silhouette Intimate Moments, and our authors keep responding by writing books that excite, amaze and compel. If you don't believe me, just take a look RaeAnne Thayne's *Nothing To Lose,* the second of THE SEARCHERS, her ongoing miniseries about looking for family—and finding love.

Valerie Parv forces a new set of characters to live up to the CODE OF THE OUTBACK in her latest, which matches a sexy crocodile hunter with a journalist in danger and hopes they'll *Live To Tell.* Kylie Brant's contribution to FAMILY SECRETS: THE NEXT GENERATION puts her couple *In Sight of the Enemy,* a position that's made even scarier because her heroine is pregnant—with the hero's child! Suzanne McMinn's amnesiac hero had *Her Man To Remember,* and boy, does *he* remember *her*—because she's the wife he'd thought was dead! Lori Wilde's heroine is *Racing Against the Clock* when she shows up in Dr. Tyler Fresno's E.R., and now his heart is racing, too. Finally, cross your fingers that there will be a *Safe Passage* for the hero and heroine of Loreth Anne White's latest, in which an agent's "baby-sitting" assignment turns out to be unexpectedly dangerous—and passionate.

Enjoy them all, then come back next month for more of the most excitingly romantic reading around—only in Silhouette Intimate Moments.

Yours,

Leslie J. Wainger

Leslie J. Wainger
Executive Editor

Please address questions and book requests to:
Silhouette Reader Service
U.S.: 3010 Walden Ave., P.O. Box 1325, Buffalo, NY 14269
Canadian: P.O. Box 609, Fort Erie, Ont. L2A 5X3

Her Man
To Remember

SUZANNE McMINN

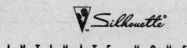

INTIMATE MOMENTS™
Published by Silhouette Books
America's Publisher of Contemporary Romance

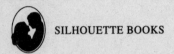 **SILHOUETTE BOOKS**

ISBN 0-373-27394-0

HER MAN TO REMEMBER

Copyright © 2004 by Suzanne McMinn

This edition published by arrangement with Harlequin Books S.A.

Visit Silhouette Books at www.eHarlequin.com

Printed in U.S.A.

Books by Suzanne McMinn

Silhouette Intimate Moments

Her Man To Remember #1324

Silhouette Romance

Make Room for Mommy #220
The Bride, the Trucker and the Great Escape #1274
The Billionaire and the Bassinet #1384

SUZANNE McMINN

Suzanne McMinn lives on a lake in North Carolina with a bunch of dogs, cats, ducks and kids. Visit her Web site at www.SuzanneMcMinn.com to learn more about her books.

With appreciation to Julie Barrett, Susan Litman,
Leslie Wainger and especially Shannon Godwin.
And of course, to MLFF—you know who you are.

Chapter 1

He'd been in Thunder Key exactly four hours and thirty-two minutes when he first saw her.

On that first day at the Shark and Fin, Roman Bradshaw hadn't believed his eyes. He'd left the beachside bar and grill without touching his drink. He'd gone back to the bungalow he'd rented—the same bungalow where they'd spent their honeymoon more than two years ago—and almost convinced himself he'd gone crazy.

The second day he made eye contact with her. She was behind the bar. Her blond hair was short; the same as always. Chin length, sexy, sassy, it swished forward onto her high cheekbones. She looked up at him from beneath the wispy bangs and met his eyes. No flicker of recognition. Nothing. Just…wide-open eyes.

A scar along her hairline, above one temple, thin, pale, was barely visible but familiar. The same silver bracelet encircled her wrist. It was a bracelet she'd worn ever since he'd given it to her on their honeymoon. And he knew it was etched with the name Leah.

He was in the back of the bar, near the door. There was a part of him that feared if he moved closer, too close, she'd disappear.

So he watched her.

She wasn't his server. But when he caught her eyes across the bar, she stared at him for a very long moment. Then she turned to the girl approaching the bar, said something to her and pointed to him.

The girl came back to his table. "Can I help you? Do you need another beer?"

He shook his head. He couldn't speak right away. Leah was still watching him but not as though she knew him. Her look was concerned, as if she was worried something was wrong.

"I'm fine, everything's fine," he had said finally, then left soon after.

He didn't know what to think. How could she not recognize him? There was nothing different about him. He wore khaki shorts and a loose, untucked tropical-print shirt he'd picked up at one of the touristy shops in Thunder Key, but other than that, he was the same Roman on the outside. The same man she'd married. It was *inside* where he'd changed.

Was it really Leah? He was afraid to find out, afraid to lose her all over again. He spent hours walking the blustery beach, his mind filled with questions he was afraid to ask. Was he losing his mind? Was the woman a figment of his imagination, a ghost walking through the nightmare his life had become since the stormy night his wife's car had gone over a bridge?

If it *was* Leah, how had she come to be here? Why had she disappeared? How could she have done this to him, to her own friends?

He dreamed of her that second night. In his dream they were driving through an autumn forest in upstate New York, enjoying the fall leaves. It was something they'd actually done on their six-month anniversary— before everything had gone wrong.

Except, in his dream, when he glanced from the road to look at his beautiful, vibrant, laughing wife and reached out to touch her, the seat beside him was suddenly empty. She'd vanished right before his eyes.

He woke, gasping for air, sweating.

The next day he arrived at the Shark and Fin earlier than usual. She wasn't there. The bar was almost empty. It was early afternoon, and outside the August sun bore down on the blazing-white beach. Vacationers straggled along the shore, carrying towels and bottles of lotion and sun umbrellas. Thunder Key was a small, offbeat island, one of the least-visited of the Florida Keys, overshadowed by its more trendy cousins—Key Largo and Key West. It boasted a quaint dot of a town off Route 1, the Overseas Highway linking the chain of coral islands to the mainland. The relative quiet, compared to more fashionable destinations, was what had appealed to Leah for their honeymoon.

Thunder Key was small, artsy, homey. There was only one hotel, and it was one of the few islands that actually maintained more permanent residents in the summer than tourists. The Shark and Fin was an outpost of local color, down a nameless road at the far end of the island. Over a humpback bridge, the Bahamian-style building suddenly appeared on the beach, as if it had emerged from the sea. Colorful fish and bright moons and carefree slogans—like, This Is As Dressed Up As I Get!—were painted on the walls. People walked in barefoot.

Leah had discovered the bar the last day of their honeymoon and she'd loved it instantly. *This is what the Keys are all about,* she'd told him. *Let's throw it all away and open a bar of our own. We could be happy here, you'll see. No stress, no smog, no cell phones or computers or fax machines. Just you and me.*

Now here he was. No cell phone. No computer. And unbelievably, Leah was here, too.

"Can I get you anything?"

Jarred from his memories, Roman looked up at the owner of the voice.

He was a young guy. He had longish blond hair, a scruffy chin and an apron around his waist. Roman had seen him come back and forth from the kitchen the past few nights. He figured he was the cook.

Although the Shark and Fin had a typical Keys menu of fried fish sandwiches, hand-cut fries, conch fritters and chowder, Roman ordered a beer. When the guy came back, he stopped him.

"I was just wondering," he began, "who owns this place?"

"Morrie Sanders." The guy gave him a look. "Is there a problem? You need to talk to Morrie? He's out west, with his daughter. Leah's in charge while he's gone, but she's not downstairs yet."

"She lives over the bar?" Roman guessed. He hadn't realized there was an apartment over the bar. Then it hit him. "Leah? Her name is Leah?"

He heard a rushing sound in his head, realized it was his pulse pounding. He hadn't imagined it. It was Leah, with her scar and her bracelet and her crooked Leah smile....

The cook's brow furrowed, and when he spoke Roman heard him as if he was very far away. "That's right." He crossed his arms. "Is something wrong?"

"No, nothing's wrong." Everything was wrong. Roman's mind reeled. *Leah.* "Leah. Is she— How long has she been here? Do you know where she's from? Do you know—"

The guy cut him off.

"Hey, do you know her or something?" He sounded protective, fierce. His whole face turned cold.

Roman backtracked. "I was just curious." He had to think fast. Leah hadn't recognized him—or at least she'd seemed not to have recognized him. He should play it casual, but he was still having a hard time thinking. "I was— She's a very attractive woman. I'm here on vacation. I thought—"

"You thought wrong."

"Can you tell me her last name?" He still couldn't believe it. Leah. Alive. Here.

"I don't give out personal information about Leah." The cook gave him a look, then turned around and walked away.

Realizing that the staff of the Shark and Fin were going to be a dead end in terms of learning about Leah, Roman went into the town. Blocks of crisscrossing, narrow, palm-shaded residential streets surrounded the backbone of the tiny Key, the main road that led to the Overseas Highway. He asked careful questions at the small grocery, the bank, the post office, the tourist office, the library and the Cuban coffeehouse. He learned she went by the name Leah Wells, that Morrie Sanders was trying to sell the Shark and Fin so he could move to New Mexico and be with his grandkids and that Leah Wells had been working for him for more than a year. It was apparent she had quickly become well liked on Thunder Key, and personal questions about her were not welcome.

He pretended he was interested in the Shark and Fin. He was a businessman from New York, he told them, and he was looking to invest in a business in the Keys.

Talk to Leah, they said. She could put him in touch with Morrie.

He wasn't ready to talk to her yet. He was afraid to talk to her, still afraid he would break the spell and she would disappear. But he had to know more about her, so he followed her. He found that in the mornings she ran on the beach. Like most residents she walked—or sometimes in her case, ran—everywhere she went on the two-mile-wide island. Then she went into town and purchased a café con leche at the Cuban coffeehouse. One morning she went into a boardwalk boutique, part of a circle of shops surrounding a shady courtyard. He discovered she sold some of her designs there. She was still making one-of-a-kind clothes—sexy dresses, barely-there tops, wild-print shorts and pants. He found she made jewelry now, too. Shell necklaces and beaded bracelets. According to the locals, her work was popular with tourists.

She spent the rest of her time at the Shark and Fin. This was her new life, the one she'd taken up after disappearing over a bridge eighteen months ago. This was Leah Wells, who didn't recognize him.

He left town and went back to the Shark and Fin. They were busy, but Roman wasn't going to sit in the back this time. He took the last open place at the bar.

When the cook came out of the kitchen, he wiped his hands on his apron and said something to Leah that Roman couldn't hear. It was then that Leah looked down the bar toward Roman.

Tonight she wore a sleeveless blouse and loose-fitting cotton pants. They were colorful—blue-and-yellow patterned. It was like Leah to wear loud clothes. They were probably her own design. They were cut to show off her slender, shapely form.

She walked toward him. "Can I help you?"

Roman's mouth went dry, his heart constricted. Her voice. Husky, low, sweet. *Leah.* He had to force himself to speak, to risk breaking the magic spell or dream or fantasy—whatever it was that had brought her back into his life. He had to find out if she was real.

"Hello, Leah." He managed to speak in a steady voice.

She didn't vanish. But her face held no expression as she stared at him. "Would you like a beer?"

Her eyes were wide open, the same as before. No recognition.

He had to know.

"Do you remember—" His heart was in his throat.

"Remember what?" She looked confused.

"—me?" he finished quietly.

"Um, I saw you here the other night." Her voice wavered into wariness. "A couple of nights, actually."

Either she was the best actress he'd ever seen, or she really didn't know who he was. He felt as if he'd been kicked in the stomach and at the same time as if the world was opening up all over again.

"You want a beer?" she asked again.

"No."

She started to turn away.

"Wait."

Her shoulders tensed. She turned back. The noise of people talking, glasses clinking, seemed to fade into the background.

"I just…want to talk to you," he said.

"I don't have time to talk." She gave a pointed glance around the bar.

"Then maybe we can talk after you close. What time is that?"

"I can't," she said. "I go to bed then."

"Then, in the morning," he countered. "I'll run with you."

Her eyes narrowed. "How do you know that I run in the morning?"

"I've seen you."

"Look," she said, her eyes cool, "I don't know what you're thinking, but I'm not interested."

"If you don't know what I'm thinking, how do you know you're not interested?"

"Joey told me— He said you were asking questions about me. That you said I was—"

"Attractive," he supplied.

She shrugged.

He *had* to speak to her.

"Give me a few minutes, that's all. I need to talk to you," he persisted.

"I can't."

"Why not?"

In Manhattan, he would have walked away a long time ago. He never asked a woman out twice if she rebuffed him. He wasn't a pursuer. But he couldn't walk away from Leah.

He knew little—actually, nothing—about memory loss. He'd called his sister Gen's husband, Mark Davison, the day before. Mark was a physician. He'd been surprised by Roman's questions but had answered them in a general way.

Memory loss could be physical or psychological. Short- or long-term. Permanent or temporary. Forcing too much information too soon on the patient could be dangerous. But Mark was a pain specialist, not a psychiatrist, he reminded Roman. He didn't have all the answers.

Why the questions? Mark had asked. But Roman had hung up without answering. He'd asked Mark not to tell Gen about the phone call. He wasn't ready to tell anyone about Leah.

"I don't date," Leah said finally.

"Why not?" He kept his tone light. She tucked her hair behind her ear. He recognized the familiar gesture. He was making her nervous.

"I'm a lesbian, all right?"

Roman almost burst out laughing. "I don't think so," he said. His mind rushed with images. Leah playing footsie with him in front of the fire—wearing nothing but socks. Leah pulling him behind a barn for a roll in the hay—at a farm where they had stopped for a wagon ride. Leah crying out during sex—at his parents' home. She was the most uninhibited, passionate sex partner he'd ever had.

"Who are you?" she demanded now, and the look in her eyes stopped him short.

Fear. She was afraid—of what? Him? He felt cold all over. What the hell had happened that night she'd gone over that bridge? Why had she been there? He'd never understood that. She'd been on a highway she didn't normally travel, on a trip she'd told no one about, carrying divorce papers he would never have signed. It had just been one of the many strange, horrible things about her death.

Finding the car had taken them two harrowing days. Inside, they'd discovered her purse, with her wedding ring tucked into a side pocket, and divorce papers inside a briefcase—but no body. They said her body had been washed away in the rain-swollen river. The search had gone on for interminable days, but divers had found nothing.

Leah had no family. The people from her design studio, already devastated by the recent loss of another artist in the co-op, had held a small memorial service.

Roman had told no one about the divorce papers. His family's relationship with Leah had been difficult enough while she had been alive. There was no point in making it worse after her death.

But she wasn't dead.

"I'm Roman," he said, watching her. Nothing. Still not a flicker. "Roman Bradshaw."

"Well, nice to meet you, Roman Bradshaw," she said, "but if you don't mind, we're busy tonight." She turned away.

He let her go because he had no choice. He couldn't

tell her the truth yet. She wasn't ready. She didn't know him, and she didn't want to know him. He couldn't just waltz in here and claim her like a caveman throwing his woman over his shoulder.

But he wasn't leaving, either.

Leah laced up her running shoes on the stoop outside the back door of the Shark and Fin. Dawn was breaking over the Atlantic. The sun shone a muted blue-gold glow through the morning clouds. It was chilly this early, but soon it would be hot.

The beach was quiet, empty. She loved this time of day, loved this beach, loved her life on Thunder Key.

She never wanted to leave, and she could only wonder, if she dared, what had taken her so long to get here. But she didn't dare. She just lived her life, one day at a time. Thunder Key was her heart and soul—the endless water, sun, sand, the laidback lifestyle and friendly people.

Thunder Key was her home, and the people here her family. It was all she knew. And as if she had come desperate, thirsting, straight from the desert, she drank in what the quaint island offered. There was not a second of the past eighteen months on Thunder Key that was not stored precisely, vividly, in her memory.

Which made the fact that she could remember nothing before then that much more startling.

Do you remember me?

The man's face leaped into her mind. Did she remember him? How could she forget him? Square jaw, intense blue eyes, planed cheeks, thick dark hair and a gorgeous, sexy dimple she'd glimpsed when he'd laughed. He was tall, wide-shouldered. Wealthy, too, she guessed. He had the bearing of a man accustomed to ordering the world to do his bidding. She'd asked around and learned he was staying in a bungalow at the White Seas Hotel, indefinitely.

The attraction had been instant, like being hit by a tidal wave. She had looked across the bar and her heart had gone wild, thumping and pounding. She'd had the insane urge to leap over the bar, throw herself into his arms, and—

What? The same way she'd known instant attraction, she had known instant fear, though she had no idea why.

But if she had learned anything in the past eighteen months, it had been to go with her instincts. Her instincts were all she had.

For example, she didn't like peas. Cats made her sneeze. And the heart-stoppingly sexy man from the White Seas was dangerous. So she had schooled her features to reflect nothing of her thoughts, and she had stayed as far away from him as possible.

Quickly she looked around now and was relieved to see no one. He knew she ran in the mornings, he'd told her that. *I need to talk to you.*

She didn't want to talk to him. She *shouldn't* talk to him.

She stood, shoes laced tightly, images flashing through her mind. The man from the night before— smiling, watching, mixed with other, stranger images of the same man, another time, another place—then he was gone and there were no more images, only sensations, sounds. They were the markers of her panic attacks.

She'd had attacks like this before—both sleeping

and waking—but not for a while. They had been so painful, so terrifying, that at first she'd thrown up after them.

Then she'd learned to block them. She had stopped trying to remember the past. And the panic attacks had vanished.

But they were back.

Rushing wind. Cold. Darkness. Screaming—her own.

Pain streaked through her temples, almost bending her double. She couldn't give in to it. She forced herself to straighten, to walk. Then run, run. Breathe. Run.

She had been a runner in her life before Thunder Key; she knew that. She could run for miles. It was her salvation from the pain, from the past. She reached the packed wet sand and she immediately found the contact soothing. She loved to run right along the shoreline. The faster she ran, the faster she could shut down the haunting bits of the past that never came together, only remained in shards that stabbed at her mind.

Somehow the man from the bar had brought the past crashing down on her again. Was that why he was dangerous? Did he remind her of someone from her past?

Or was he someone from her past?

Birds wheeled overhead, their calls breaking the still morning air. She was alone, all alone, but in her head the haunting wind and screams played on. Sometimes she was afraid she was going crazy.

I know who you are, the voice said. Who was she?

Run, run, run. Before her head exploded.

I know what you've done. What terrible thing had she done? Why? What kind of person was she? Did she even want to know?

Leah ran faster, faster. Running was the first thing she remembered.

Pitch-black night, lights flashing past, air, just air, and she was dropping, dropping, dropping. Water. Pain. But not so terrible. No, she could move. She could run.

The trucker who had picked her up from the side of the highway had worn a green-checkered shirt and faded blue jeans with a hole over one knee. He had a round, easy face, and kind eyes.

"I'm going south," he'd said.

"Me, too," she'd answered. "Thunder Key."

Where had that come from? She hadn't even known where Thunder Key was located. It had come out of nowhere, and it had actually scared her, but everything had scared her that night, so she hadn't let that stop her.

She'd been damp, bruised, shaken. Barely dawn, and she hadn't known how long she'd been running.

"You got a name?" the trucker had asked.

She hadn't known what to say. The trucker had reached over, and in the glow of the rig's dash, had touched the bracelet on her arm.

"Leah." He'd read the engraved letters. "You got a last name?"

They'd passed an interstate sign: Wells, 1 Mile.

"Leah...Wells." She'd shivered in the heated cab.

He'd had a road atlas. In the index, she'd found Thunder Key, part of the chain of islands that appeared like an afterthought on the tip of the Florida coast.

The trucker had taken her as far as South Carolina. He'd given her money for a bus ticket from Charles ton. He'd insisted.

"A pretty lady like you shouldn't be hitching," he'd said.

She'd made him give her his home address, and promised to send him the money. And she'd sent it, a month later, after she'd gotten her first paycheck from the Shack and Pier.

She'd met Morrie on the beach the day she'd arrived on Thunder Key. She'd been sitting on a bench, just staring out at the vast ocean of clear water.

"Are you lost?" he'd asked her.

"No. I think I'm found." She was where she'd meant to go. That was all she knew.

Then he'd asked her if she needed a job and a place to live. He didn't ask any more questions after that. He didn't care where she came from. At a trim and vigorous sixty, the slightly balding bar owner didn't like to talk about his own past, but she knew he'd been in prison. He was reformed, he told her. He'd started life over in Thunder Key.

She knew he must have still had connections. He'd offered to help her dig into her past after she confided in him that she'd lost her memory. And one day he'd shown up with an array of identification for Leah Wells.

"In case you ever need it," he'd told her.

She hadn't liked taking the false ID, but she hadn't wanted to hurt his feelings. He'd done so much for her. So she had put the documents away in a drawer.

Recently he'd reconciled with the family from

which he'd been long estranged. Leah missed him, and she wondered what the future held for her.

For eighteen months she'd been happy here. Now Morrie was selling the bar, and a stranger was watching her.

And the panic attacks were back.

She stopped running when she came to the public beach and the parking lot outside the community center. From there she walked up Thunder Key's main street, letting her breathing slow as she headed for the coffeehouse.

The town was quiet in the early mornings. In the distance she could see a car or two on the Overseas Highway. Most drivers kept right on going, heading for the hot spots of the other islands where they could find more exciting attractions and hipper nightlife.

Thunder Key suited Leah just fine. Just as she'd known it would.

She had her breathing and her nerves under control by the time she reached the counter inside the just-opened-for-the-day coffeehouse.

"Hi, Viv," she said. "Got my café con leche ready?"

"Of course," Vivien Ramon said, her rough smoker's voice softened by her smile and the youthful sparkle in her eyes that belied the silver threading through her swing of rich black hair. Her husband was a sail maker, and Viv ran La Greca, the island's only coffeehouse. If Morrie was like a father to Leah, then Viv was like a mother.

Her real parents were dead. She just knew that, without question.

Like Morrie, Viv didn't ask too many questions. But Leah knew Viv worried about her.

Viv had wanted her to see a doctor. Like Morrie, she'd offered to help Leah find out about her past. So far, Leah had held back. She was afraid—of what, she didn't know. But she knew her past held pain, and that was enough to stop her from seeking answers. She wasn't ready, she'd told them both.

Maybe she'd never be ready.

"Here you go, honey," Viv said, handing the sweet, hot espresso across the counter. Then she was looking beyond Leah.

"I'll have what she's having."

Leah nearly leaped out of her skin, but she managed to stay very still. Then, slowly, very slowly, she forced herself to turn.

"Good morning," he said, and his smile suggested he didn't have a care in the world.

He must have come in behind her, but she hadn't seen him outside. How had she missed him? How had she missed, for even a second, those intense, dangerous blue eyes of his? He was so devastatingly present, so vivid, just as he had been in the bar the night before.

She wanted to hate him. The reaction was strong, visceral. She couldn't explain it. She wanted to say something horrible and rude. She wanted to shout at him. *Go away!*

But it was hard to think—much less speak—with her throat blocked by her heart.

"Fancy meeting you here. Roman. Roman Bradshaw. From the bar," he clarified unnecessarily.

Leah finally found her tongue. "Yes, of course. Ro-

man.'' His name came across her lips smoothly, and
she felt very strange, shivery, as she said it. She picked
up her coffee and avoided meeting Viv's eyes, though
she didn't miss the curious look on her friend's face.

When Viv wasn't offering to set her up with a physician, she was offering to set her up with a date.

But Leah wasn't ready for that, either. She had rebuffed Viv's every well-intentioned attempt. And
she'd had no regrets.

Her heart had felt so dead all this time.

But right now, her heart was hammering like mad.

''I need to talk to you,'' the man named Roman
said. Then, ''Thank you,'' to Viv, taking the second
cup she handed across the counter.

''I don't see what we have to talk—'' Leah began,
then stopped short.

As she watched him, he paid for his and hers, she
realized suddenly.

''No,'' she said sharply, pulling herself together. ''I
don't want you to—''

''It's no problem,'' he said. ''Forget it.''

Leah pulled out the exact change she carried with
her in the pocket of her windbreaker every morning
and placed it on the counter.

She barged past him toward the door.

A woman came through the door, a small black poodle on a leash at her side. Leah, limbs trembling for
no good reason, strode blindly, wanting—needing—to
get out of the suddenly too-small coffeehouse. And
tripped right over the dog.

The poodle yelped, Leah went down and coffee flew
everywhere. She swore and apologized, and pretended
the coffee hadn't burned the hell out of her fingers.

"Are you all right?" Roman was instantly at her side.

Viv handed him towels. She already had a mop. The woman with the poodle was wiping her sleeve where some coffee had splattered her. The poodle yipped and danced, its perfectly painted toenails clattering on the tile floor.

"I'm fine. I'm sorry," Leah said to Viv. "I'll pay your cleaning bill," she told the woman. "Send it to me at the Shark and Fin. I'm sorry," she said again, in general.

Then she was on her feet and hit the door without another word. She was on the sidewalk before she knew it.

"Wait."

Not a chance.

"You should take care of those hands," he said. "They'll blister."

Roman caught up with her, his long, lean strides no match for her somewhat shorter legs. She could run, but she'd just bet he would keep up with her.

"They're fine. I'm fine." She refused to look at him, but she was aware of him just the same.

He even smelled good, damn him. Soapy, musky, all male.

Danger, danger. Red lights, stop signs, railroad crossing bars. She had to get away from him.

"Would you slow down?"

She whirled. "Would you stop following me?" she demanded. "Didn't I make it clear last night that I don't want to talk to you?"

"If you don't talk to me, then how is Morrie going to sell me his bar?" he answered matter-of-factly.

For a minute she could only stare at him. "You're interested in the bar?" Could she be a bigger idiot?

She thought of how she'd behaved in the coffee-house, how she'd raced out of there. She'd been practically in a frenzy.

"I'm sorry," she said. "It's just—" How did she explain? He was a stranger. She didn't even tell her—brief—life story to people she saw every day. Viv and Morrie were the only ones who knew the whole story. Even Joey, the cook at the Shark and Fin, only knew part of it.

"Just what?" he prompted.

"You remind me of someone," she said finally. "I don't…" This question terrified her. What if he didn't just remind her of someone? What if he was someone she'd known? Unable to avoid it any longer, she finally asked, "I don't know you, do I?"

She felt as if her stomach had fallen to her feet while she waited.

Chapter 2

"No," he said very quietly, watching her. "You don't know me."

Leah swallowed thickly. "I'm sorry," she said for about the tenth time in the past ten minutes. "I guess I was just... I don't know."

"Nothing to be sorry about," he said briskly. "Why don't we start over?" He held out his hand.

God, could he be more cool, more self-possessed, more hellaciously good-looking? *Danger, danger.*

"Start over?" she asked, trying to get her thoughts under control.

"I'm Roman Bradshaw," he said again. He still had his hand out. "I'm from New York. I'm looking to invest in a business in the Keys. I'm interested in Morrie's bar."

She took his hand. Electricity shot all the way up her arm, and it was all she could do not to yank her hand back.

"I'm Leah. Leah Wells." She sounded almost normal, thank God. "I'm taking care of the bar for Morrie. I'd be happy to provide you with any information—"

He hadn't let go of her hand. The electrical pulses hadn't stopped coming, either. And simply being this close to him was making her knees shake.

"Good," he said. "I'm free this morning, if you have time for me."

There was something unguarded in his expression. His burningly intense eyes seared her still, but she realized there was a vulnerability there, too.

"The bar opens at ten," she said, quaking inside with unnamed emotions. "Meet me then." She withdrew her hand and walked away, but she knew he didn't move, that he watched her all the way down the street to the beach.

The water glittered in a kaleidoscope of blues and greens, light reflecting up from the bottom of the ocean. Graceful sea birds glided and dipped. It was a sight she loved, craved to drink in each morning. But for the first time, she was in a rush to get back to the bar.

She felt his gaze long after she knew she was out of sight. She took the stairs in the back hall of the bar by twos and went straight to the shower. With water pouring down over her face, she cried for no reason at all.

"Darling, I just pray that you will find the same kind of happiness that Genevieve and Mark have. You know that's all I care about. All I think about. Your happiness. You simply must come home."

Roman held the bungalow phone in his tense, impatient hand, listening to his mother try to convince him to return to New York. He'd come back to the White Seas after seeing Leah at the coffeehouse, biding his time till their scheduled meeting at the Shark and Fin. He needed a few moments to collect his thoughts, calm his pounding heart.

He didn't need this conversation with his mother.

"We miss you," Barbara Bradshaw continued. "You need us."

"I need Thunder Key," Roman said plainly. "This is where I want to be, where I need to be right now."

"What good can come of wallowing in that girl's death?" his mother demanded, her voice breaking.

" 'That girl' was my wife, Mother. Leah. She had a name." *Is* my wife, he corrected to himself. *Has* a name.

He hadn't told his mother about seeing Leah. Even after eighteen months of thinking Leah was dead, his family hadn't softened their attitude toward her. They wouldn't gladly accept her back, and his gut instincts told him they would attempt to convince him that her memory loss was some kind of fraud. Hadn't they tried, over and over, to find a way to tear him and Leah apart? They never had.

He'd destroyed their marriage all by himself.

After she'd been declared dead, he'd gone back to work. His work had always been so important to him. His grandfather had been the founder of Bradshaw Securities, a professional trading firm. It was a family business—his father, his uncles, his cousins, his sister. It had always been assumed that Roman would take his father's place as the CEO and chairman of the board someday. But now it was all so empty. Stocks, bonds, trading options. Who cared?

His apartment with a view of Central Park was empty, too. No Leah, lacing up her running shoes, daring him to keep up with her.

No Leah, cooking another awful meal and sneaking in takeout at the last minute.

No Leah, dancing in her underwear in front of the couch until he turned off his laptop and paid attention to her instead.

At least, that was how things had started out. Gradually she'd realized he wasn't going to change, and that the very thing that had drawn them together—their utter dissimilarity—could also pull them apart. He didn't know how it had happened. It was as if he'd looked up one day from his eighty-hour workweek and he'd lost her, and he didn't know how to get her back.

Then there was no getting her back because she was dead.

He'd spent the first three months afterward pretending nothing had happened. Then he spent another year pretending he could deal with it.

The last three months, he'd given up the farce. He'd stopped going in to the office. His family had gone into shock. His father had raised Roman to take over the firm from the time he was born. Roman's first memory was of his father bringing him to Wall Street to hear the opening bell rung when he was four years old. He earned a business degree from 'Yale and an MBA from Harvard.

He'd walked away from a multimillion-dollar legacy, and he still wasn't sure why. He'd closed up his Central Park apartment. He'd put dustcovers on the furniture, protective bags over his business suits. He'd cleared every commitment from his always-full date-book.

It had taken three months for him to undo the life in New York he'd thought was more important to him than anything, even his wife.

His family thought they were watching their golden boy lose it.

"Mother, I have to go," he said, bringing his thoughts back to the present.

"But when will you be back in New York?"

"I don't know when I'm coming back. In fact, I'm thinking about making an investment here, a bar called the Shark and Fin. So don't expect me back right away and don't worry about me. I'm fine. I'm doing business." If anything would convince his family he was fine, it was the idea that he was making an investment—though they probably wouldn't be thrilled it was in Thunder Key. He said goodbye and hung up before his mother could get in another word.

He stared out the open garden doors of the bungalow. Beyond lay a perfect, picture-postcard world. White sands, blue ocean, clear sky. He closed his eyes, let the palm fronds rustling in the ocean breeze take him away....

Leah danced out the garden doors, silhouetted against the barely dawn blue-gold world. "Come on, you're too slow!"

He told her to wait. He was shaving. She tickled him. He laughed, but kept shaving. "I can't wait. I hope you can catch me—before someone else does!" She disappeared.

Roman dropped his razor, ran out of the bungalow

wearing nothing but a towel. Leah could do that to him, make him do crazy things that didn't come naturally to his conservative, subdued, Bradshaw personality. He raced across the empty, secluded beach, holding on to the towel and his dignity just barely, and caught up with her in the water—or maybe she caught him because somehow she was in his arms, her legs wrapped around his waist.

They fell into the shallow sea together, her sparkling green eyes his only contact with the world, and then somehow his towel disappeared and her bikini bottoms slipped away…and she had him doing things in the dawn-misted surf that were very un-Bradshaw-like indeed—

Roman opened his eyes, gasped. How could it still hurt so much? How could he still miss her so deeply? How could he still feel her in his arms?

Unable to keep his mind off her, he went straight to the Shark and Fin. He was early, but he couldn't wait any longer. He walked, taking the boardwalk trail through a mangrove-lined lagoon that stood between the resort hotel and the town. He'd rented a car after flying in to Key West airport, but since he'd arrived on Thunder Key, he hadn't touched it.

As he came out of the grove and into the town, he turned down the narrow, overgrown road that led to the Shark and Fin. Beyond the beachside bar and grill, he saw dolphins jumping in the brilliant blue water.

Dolphins mean good luck, Leah had told him when they'd seen dozens of them dancing up out of the waves during a seaplane tour of the Keys.

He hoped she was right. He could use some luck.

The Shark and Fin was just opening for the day.

The front door was open to the fresh air and rapidly warming morning. Ceiling fans moved the lazy air as Leah sat at a scarred oak table by a large window, her fingers racing over a sketch pad. Her eyes were intensely focused on her creation.

Roman stopped in the doorway, just taking her in with his eyes, his heart. How many times had he caught her in the exact same pose, working on one of her designs in their apartment in the city? Memories washed over him and he could barely breathe for a moment. He knew he couldn't speak yet.

She'd showered since her run—her hair was still damp on the ends. Leah had always been too impatient to get on with her day to blow-dry her hair. Her makeup was minimal—also as usual—just enough to highlight her glossy lips, outline her remarkable eyes, trace her high cheekbones. She wore a hot-pink sleeveless tank top and capri bottoms in white. She swung one sandaled foot while she worked, and he noticed that her toes were painted with little hot-pink smiley-faces.

She was oblivious to him, lost in her work.

But he wasn't oblivious to her. His pulse had shot into overdrive as soon as he'd laid eyes on her, and the past swamped him again.

You remind me of someone. He'd been hard-pressed not to blurt out everything when she'd said those words to him. *I don't know you, do I?* What was he supposed to say, to do? His heart screamed for him to pull her into his arms and tell her she belonged to him, they were husband and wife, she was his Leah, dammit.

No. You don't know me. His words had been true—
she *didn't* know him. Not yet.

But she would, in time. Take it slow, that's what he
kept telling himself. Slow, slow, slow.

It was killing him. But he was scared, so scared, of
losing her all over again. What if she remembered
him—and didn't want him? It was she who'd had divorce papers drawn up—not him. Had it been some
kind of last-ditch attempt to shake him into changing,
into noticing her, into putting her first?

"Hi," he said quietly, coming forward into the bar
now, finally recovering his voice.

Startled, she looked up at him. As their eyes met, it
was as if he heard the surf roar straight into the bar
and he felt himself drowning all over again.

"Oh, hi," she said, scraping her chair back and
standing to greet him. She dropped the sketch pad and
pencil to hold out her hand, very businesslike, but he
didn't miss the nervous tuck she gave her hair, pushing
it back behind her ear.

She gave him her all-too-familiar crooked smile,
and that alone nearly made him lose it.

Then she surprised him by blushing as their hands
met. She had a shy side, this new Leah. For all that
was the same, there were so many differences, and he
wanted to know all of them. He had to know everything about her new life.

"Thank you for meeting with me this morning," he
said smoothly, letting go of her hand despite every
shouting fiber of his being that wanted him to do the
opposite, to pull her all the way into his arms, hold
her and never let go. But rushing Leah was probably

the worst thing he could do if he didn't want to lose her again.

He had to file his red-hot longing for her in the same place where he had kept the grief and guilt of losing her for the past eighteen months.

"I've been in touch with Morrie," she said. "He suggested I give you a tour of the bar, then if you're still interested, I'll put through a call to him and let you two hash out the details."

"Great," Roman said agreeably. He'd already decided to buy the bar. He didn't need to know the details. Hell, he'd buy the whole island if he had to.

The tour didn't take long. The bar itself was wide-open, airy, bright with the morning light pouring in. There was the requisite back room with a pool table, and the small kitchen where the cook whipped up conch chowder and fried catch-of-the-day, along with a few other simple short-order items.

"Can I see upstairs?" he asked.

He knew it was an intimate request since she lived in the upstairs apartment, but it would be his, of course, if he purchased the bar. He had every right to see it.

He wanted to see where she lived.

She appeared to hesitate, then she said, "Sure."

He thought he saw a hint of blush tinge her cheeks again. She led the way up the narrow, cramped back stairs.

"This is it," she said, opening the door and standing out of the way.

He walked past her into the room. Against one wall, a counter, sink and stove made up the kitchen. A Murphy bed took up another wall, but she hadn't put it up, and the twisted sheets and piled pillows made his chest tighten. The entire apartment was characteristically Leah-messy. He noticed she had walked to the large window. She stood there, framed by light sheers that left the ocean view uncluttered, except for a strange concoction of branches, suede lacing, beads and feathers that hung down in the center.

The rest of the room was taken up by a small dinette with two chairs and a plump tan love seat with a round coffee table. She grew a pot of overflowing ivy and miniature sunflowers in the center of it. Spare sketch pads and pencils, a couple of books and magazines and a box of shells and thread for her jewelry loaded up every spare inch of space around the plants.

"You're an artist?" he inquired casually.

She turned to face him. "I design a few things— clothes, jewelry," she said.

Her designs had been sold in expensive boutiques in Manhattan. She had been just as self-effacing about her work then.

Leah had never taken herself seriously. She could have made a fortune; but she'd never operated that way. The demand for her work had always been much higher than her production. She wasn't lazy—on the contrary, she worked very hard. But she hadn't been willing to let it consume her.

It had been just one of the ways they'd approached life differently.

"You're a very creative person," he commented. He was all-business, conservative. *Maybe we were never meant to be,* she'd told him once when they were fighting. *We're too different.*

"You haven't even seen my work."

"I'd like to see your work," he said, covering quickly. "Is it showcased here on the island somewhere?"

Of course, he'd already seen her recent work displayed on the boardwalk. The day he'd been there, a reggae band was performing for free in the courtyard. Beyond, the public beach offered dive shops and snorkeling gear rentals. A sign in front of the marina advertised a bucket of fish for a dollar to tourists who wanted to feed the pelicans and huge tarpons swarming below the dock.

He'd fed the fish and watched Leah from the distance as she entered a boutique.

"There's a small shopping center on Rum Beach," she said. "It's called Smugglers Village. You can see my work there in the Artisans Cove boutique."

"Maybe you could show it to me," he suggested, managing to sound blithe. "I haven't had a chance to see much of Thunder Key, and if I'm going to be making a property investment here, I'd like to find out more about the island first. It wouldn't be a date," he added to defuse any argument before she made it.

Again he caught her faint blush.

"I'm sorry I made such a big deal about that," she said. "I know that sounded stupid. I'm not ready to date, that's all."

"Why is that?" he asked, carefully.

She was very still, then she answered in a quiet voice, "I'm not sure. Really, I don't know why ·I'm even telling you this."

The confusion in her soft eyes hurt him.

"I know how you feel," he said gently. "I was

married, but—'' he began, then waited. For a reaction, anything—

"But what?" she prompted, her eyes wide.

One heartbeat, two. "I lost her, in an accident."

She blinked. "I'm sorry," she said, sympathy gleaming in her eyes. He even saw moisture there. She was ready to cry—for him.

Leah had always been one to respond to others' pain. Not long after they'd married, one of her friends from the studio had suffered an inoperable back injury in a car accident. Like Leah, Nikki Bates had no family, and it had been Leah who had sat by her hospital bed, visited her with food and helped her when she was finally sent home. And no one had been more crushed than Leah when Nikki overdosed on pain medication only weeks before Leah disappeared.

The suicide of someone so close to her had torn Leah apart—and it was for exactly that reason that when one of the crash investigators had tried broaching the possibility that Leah might have driven her car over that bridge on purpose, Roman had flatly dismissed it. There was just no way. Leah had been too hurt by Nikki's death to ever leave anyone else with the cruel guilt of losing someone that way.

Roman changed the subject, not ready to talk more about the past yet. Not ready to risk that she would remember him before he'd had a chance to convince her that he was a different man.

"What is this?" he said, reaching out to touch the artistic creation of beads, feathers, branches and suede in the window. There wasn't much in the apartment, so he was curious about what she would choose to display. He had to focus on getting to know this new Leah.

"It's a dreamcatcher."

"What's that?" he asked. He'd never seen anything like it.

"It's from an old Native American legend," she explained. She touched the beaded suede laces that made up a web. "The web catches the good dreams, and the hole in the center—" She put her fingers in the opening. "The bad dreams go out through here."

"Do you have bad dreams?" He stepped closer to her, wanting so much to hold her. He had to clench his fists at his sides to prevent himself from following through on the urge.

She nodded. "Yes. Sometimes."

He couldn't stop himself from asking, "About what?"

"I don't know exactly," she said softly, looking away. "I never remember much of them."

Was he the bad dream she couldn't remember?

Now it was her turn to change the subject. She took a deep breath, exhaled and looked straight at him again. "Why don't we go downstairs to Morrie's office and you can talk to him on the phone, then I'll—" She gave a light shrug, smiled her crooked, heart-destroying smile. "Maybe we can go down to the boardwalk. Joey will be in, and a couple of the waitresses. I don't have to be here till later. If you still want me to, I can show you around."

"That sounds perfect," Roman said. He forced a smile, feeling like a lying bastard in spite of all his good intentions. But he was fully prepared to keep on lying, as long as he had to.

He needed time. He needed to seduce her all over again—and this time he needed to do it right.

He'd lost Leah once, and he'd be damned if he was going to lose her again.

Chapter 3

What drugs had she been on when she'd decided this was a good idea?

Okay, she didn't do drugs. Had never done drugs. That she knew of. But Leah was pretty sure she'd been high on something when the words, *If you still want me to, I can show you around,* had popped out of her mouth.

Morrie had asked her to get to know his potential buyer. He wanted to sell the bar, but not to just anyone. He wanted to know the bar wouldn't be torn down or all the staff fired. But she hadn't had to offer to take Roman around town. It had been an impulsive, stupid idea. It wasn't even like her to be impulsive. At least, if it ever had been like her, it wasn't like her now. She was careful, cautious, wary.

But she knew what'd had her high.

Roman Bradshaw's dimple that—when he smiled—

made her think he wasn't scary at all. But it was an illusion. He *was* scary. Her strong reaction to him was proof.

And now she was stuck with him for the whole morning. Thank God they weren't alone.

Smugglers Village teemed with activity. The boardwalk included a bookstore, a sandal shop, a sportsman's paradise, the standard touristy T-shirt booth and a cozy little restaurant offering a menu of Keysy food. The Artisans Cove was full of New Age samplings like incense, candles, oils, yoga guides, along with jewelry and clothing. A number of artists showcased their work on consignment, taking turns to work in the shop. Leah manned the counter one morning a week.

"So these are yours." Roman touched a display of beaded bracelets. He'd dressed in jeans today, with a white T-shirt that clung to his shoulders and pecs. He was an eye-catching man, and she wasn't the only one who'd noticed.

The artist working the cash register had lifted her brows when they'd come in, but Marian had been helping another customer, thankfully. Leah felt uncomfortable coming into the shop with Roman. She'd made it clear to everyone she knew that she wasn't interested in dating, and she didn't want anyone to get the wrong idea now.

"Yes, those are mine," she said, then realized he'd pointed them out before she'd told him. "How did you know?"

"Just guessed," he answered easily. "They remind me of the work I saw in your apartment."

"These are mine, too." Leah pointed at another rack holding crystal and ethnic stone necklaces. "And the designs in that window.'' She indicated a clothing nook near the door. ''I use all hand-printed fabrics from a studio in Key West.''

''They're beautiful,'' Roman said. ''I'm impressed.''

His fingers were long, strong-looking, and she found herself staring at them. Wanting to touch them.

''Don't be,'' she said. ''It's nothing. It's just something I do for fun.'' She forced herself to look away from his hands, unnerved by how everything about him fascinated her, drew her and repulsed her all at once.

He turned from the jewelry counter, an intense look suddenly crossing his face. ''You always do that.''

''Always do what?'' A dizzy sensation crawled up her spine. *Do I know you?* And he'd told her no. Had he lied? How would she ever know?

''You put yourself down. You never—''

''You don't even know me. How can you say that?''

Now he was the one who looked off-kilter, and his gaze on her was odd.

''You're right.'' He looked away. ''I don't know why I said that. These are great, that's all. I gave you a compliment. Just say thank you.'' There was something suddenly sad in his face.

''Thank you,'' she said, and had a strange urge to add… What? She didn't even know.

The bell on the door clanged. The customer had left the shop. Marian hurried over. Her gaze on Roman was clearly appreciative.

Leah felt a weird twist in her chest.

''Hi, Leah.'' She was still looking at Roman.

"Marian, this is Roman Bradshaw. From New York. He's thinking of buying the Shark and Fin. I'm showing him around the Key a bit. Marian's another artist," she explained to Roman. "She's a potter."

"I see. Well, welcome to Thunder Key, Roman Bradshaw." Marian stuck her hand out and smiled flirtatiously.

Roman took her hand briefly. Marian was tall, blond, self-assured. Everything Leah was not. Dammit, was she jealous? She had never felt this way before, and she didn't like it. Marian was a sweetie, and truly, she'd been a good friend. She was the one who'd invited Leah to join the Artisans Cove group. She was single and manhunting—as Marian herself put it—and Leah had made a huge point of the fact that *she wasn't.*

But she hated how Marian was looking at Roman. It made her feel possessive and childish and ridiculous.

"Thank you," Roman said to Marian. Marian smiled.

Leah pointed out some of Marian's work, and Roman made some appreciative comments.

After a few minutes Roman said to Leah, "I noticed they sell buckets of fish at the marina. How about taking a walk out there? I'd like to discuss a few things Morrie brought up with me on the phone."

A mix of feelings tangled inside her. She was stupidly flattered that he was showing no interest in Marian whatsoever. Instead, his heavy, cloaked gaze arrowed intensely on Leah. Which was exactly why, at the same time, she felt so horribly uneasy.

"All right." What else could she say, do? As long

as they were discussing business, everything would be fine.

But it didn't feel like business when he opened the door of the shop, placed a gentle hand beneath her elbow as they walked out onto the boardwalk. Leah walked faster, moving away from his touch.

"Bye," Marian called. The bell above the shop door clanged as it shut behind them.

"She liked you," Leah forced herself to slow down enough to comment. "She's a really sweet person. If you…you know, if you're interested in having some fun, seeing the nightlife, Marian is really the person to show you around. She's a lot of fun and—"

She realized he'd stopped. She turned, looked back at him.

"Are you trying to set me up?" He seemed amused.

The reggae band was warming up. The sun beat down on the boardwalk, alive with tourists in the still-cool morning air. The underlying heat brushed her skin. Soon it would be another blazing-hot Keys day.

"No, I—" She didn't know what to say. She felt like an idiot every time she opened her mouth around this man. "You're here on vacation. I guess it's kind of a working vacation, but still… I'm sure you want to have some fun, and Marian—"

"Look, I'm not interested in Marian. And I'm not trying to come on to you, either. But if I buy the bar, we're going to be working together. You're not interested in me. You're a lesbian. I got it. You don't have to keep telling me. Maybe *you* should date Marian."

Stupider and stupider. That's how she felt. But she couldn't help laughing. "I don't think so."

"You're really starting to damage my self-esteem,"

he said, a teasing note entering his deep voice. "I'm going to need therapy if you keep telling me how much you *don't* want to date me."

He stuck his hand out.

"Friends?" he said.

She met his now-serious gaze. "Friends." She put her hand in his. There went the twist in her chest again, but what choice did she have? Morrie had been thrilled someone was interested in the bar, even if somewhat wary yet. Things were going well in New Mexico, and selling the Shark and Fin would mean he could make his move out there permanent. She owed Morrie so much.

And if I buy the bar, we're going to be working together.

How had that thought not even entered her head till now? Somehow she had just assumed—

"Wouldn't you be going back to New York? I thought this was just an investment for you?"

They left Smugglers Village, taking the boardwalk path that led to the marina. The sound of the reggae music filtered through the air.

"I plan to move here," he said.

"Oh."

"You sound disappointed. Wow, I *am* going to need therapy."

He smiled, and she was struck by the even whiteness of his teeth, and the way his dark eyes lit with mischief. There was something so contradictory about him. His entire bearing was so businesslike, reserved, and yet when he looked at her, there was a hint of vulnerability to his dark, shielded depths, and then there were those moments of lightness, not to mention those flashing dimples. She just couldn't figure him out, and she shouldn't even want to.

"No, I'm just surprised, that's all." Shocked, more like it.

"You can't see me living here on the Keys?"

"No. Well, you're from the city. You're—"

"What? You don't even know me. How can you say that?" He tossed her own words back at her with another flare of light in his enigmatic eyes.

She stopped in front of the marina, bit her lip. He was sexy, dangerous, all male. And so very close to her, his look on her so very intense.

"You're right," she said abruptly. "I don't have a right to say anything about you at all. I don't know what I was thinking."

She couldn't tell him what she was thinking.

"You're not completely wrong," he said.

She blinked. "What do you mean?"

"I'm from the city," he explained. "The life here on the Keys—it's not me. Or, it wasn't me. But things have changed. I've changed." He looked out toward the water. Something in his face struck her as terribly painful, and her heart gave another wrench in response. Was he thinking of his wife, the one he'd lost in an accident? "I *want* it to be me," he finished quietly.

She didn't want to feel anything for him at all, but the look in his eyes made her wish she was a different person, the type of person who could put her arms around him and comfort him. And really just be friends.

"Do you believe people can change?"

His question took her by surprise, as did the look

in his eyes, as if her answer truly mattered to him. Which, of course, it couldn't. Why would it?

"I don't know," she answered honestly. "I guess it depends on how much they want to."

He didn't say anything for a beat. "Come on," he said then. "Let's get a bucket."

She followed him inside the marina. He paid for a bucket of fish at the counter and they walked out to the pier. She experienced the familiar discomfort that walking over water always gave her, but managed to push past it. She still didn't like the water, avoided getting in the sea to swim, but she'd gotten used to seeing it every day. It was part of Thunder Key. The sea was beautiful, and she didn't understand her fear of it. She'd learned to live with it.

There were a few tourists, but most of the early crowd was lined up at the dive shop and snorkel shack. The air was salty and fresh and clean. Watching Roman, she had the craziest urge to tangle her fingers through his hair, as if it would be perfectly natural, and ask him to tell her why he thought he needed to change.

"So you had some questions about the bar," she said instead.

Business, business, business. She needed to talk about something that didn't make her want to put her arms around him or hold his hands or probe into the sadness behind those amazing dark eyes.

"Not questions, really. I just wanted to let you know that nothing's going to change. In case you're concerned about that. I know that's important to Morrie." He leaned over the railing, tossed a fish to the tarpons below, then looked back at her. "Morrie emphasized that he wants you to feel secure here at the bar. He really cares about you."

"Morrie's great." She settled her arms against the railing, stared down at the gathering tarpons. The water glittered in the growing day. "He's been like a father to me. But you're buying the bar, so I understand it's up to you what you do with it."

A thread of nervousness wound through her words, but like her fear of water, she'd learned to live with the new uncertainty since Morrie had put the bar up for sale. With no past, and the future unknowable, living day to day was all she could handle.

The fact was, no matter how much Morrie felt like a father to her, she wasn't his family. His family was in New Mexico, and that's where Morrie wanted to be.

"I like the Shark and Fin just the way it is," Roman said. "And the people, too. I just wanted you to know. I won't be asking you to move out of the apartment, and I'm not planning to change any of the staffing."

"You'll need a place to live," she pointed out.

"I'm fine at the White Seas for now. I'll figure out the rest of it as I go."

Apparently he had unlimited funds if he could stay at the White Seas indefinitely. It was one of the most expensive resorts in the Keys simply because it was so secluded on sleepy little Thunder Key. There was limited potential for any farther development on the island due to the environmental restrictions preserving most of the remaining natural areas on the Key.

Roman dug into the bucket and tossed another handful of fish to the tarpons. The pelicans near the pier had taken note and a couple dove toward them.

Leah took a handful and a white pelican ate straight from her fingers. Roman fed another, and half the bucket was gone in minutes.

She laughed as one pelican nipped her fingers greedily, and she looked up at Roman. He was grinning back at her.

"I like it when you laugh," he said. "You don't laugh enough."

That sobered her instantly. "Why do you want to buy a bar in the Keys?" Dammit, she hadn't meant to ask him that.

He had a way of just looking at her and sending her completely off balance.

"I honeymooned here with my wife."

It was the last thing she'd expected him to say.

"Here? On Thunder Key?"

"At the White Seas. Two years ago."

The pain in his eyes just about killed her. The urge to touch him grew almost unbearable. There was something about him that just pulled her against her will.

If he'd only been married two years ago, his wife had to have died fairly recently. And now he'd come back. It was hard for her to imagine how it must feel for him to be here. Painful, to say the least.

"I would think this is the last place you'd want to be," she said. Hide. That's what pain made her want to do. But Roman wasn't hiding. He'd come right here, to the very place that must hurt him the most. "I feel like an idiot. I was trying to set you up with Marian and I thought you were interested in me. I had no idea your loss had been so…recent. It must be difficult for you to be back here."

He leaned against the railing. "This is the only place I want to be," he said. The wind picked up, almost carrying his words away. She had to move closer to hear him. The salty air mingled with the musky male scent of him.

"I'm truly sorry for your loss," she said. What would that be like, to care so deeply—and then to lose that person? She wondered if she would ever know. If she had known in the past. It was one of the things that frightened her, to think there might be someone, somewhere, who missed her. It was one of the reasons she couldn't bring herself to date. What if she had a husband? Children? She didn't even know if she was free. But she had convinced herself that if she had a family, she would know. Somehow. Wouldn't she?

Most of the time the questions were just too awful to contemplate.

"I was a bastard," he said, surprising her again. The sharp darkness of his eyes pierced her as he cut his gaze to her again. "I wasn't a good husband during our marriage, and then it was too late. I lost her. Don't feel sorry for me. Everything that happened was my own fault."

He dug in the bucket again, tossed another handful of fish at the tarpons.

"Wow, not hard on yourself or anything, are you?" she said. "And you said I put myself down. I think you've got me beat."

"I believe in a person taking responsibility for his actions. Especially when the person was wrong."

"That's admirable, but still… It takes two people to make a marriage. You can't blame yourself entirely."

''She did,'' he said.

Leah didn't know what to say to that. ''I think if you can admit you made some mistakes, that says a lot about you. You don't strike me as a bastard.'' Nope, not at all. He was being so damn nice, she felt the shield around her peeling back with every second she spent with him. And that was bad.

Very bad.

She had nothing to offer a man like Roman Bradshaw. No past, no future, barely a present. There were solid reasons she'd made up her mind not to get involved in a relationship, and just because Roman was hellaciously good-looking and nice to boot didn't change any of it. Discovering he was a sensitive guy didn't mean he wasn't dangerous.

She needed to get things back on more solid footing. Something she could handle. ''Morrie told me to give you whatever access you need. If you want to look at the books today, I can make them available to you. I've been keeping the books and managing the bar myself since Morrie's been gone, so I can fill you in on most of the business details and any questions you might have.''

''Great.'' He threw out some more fish and neither of them said anything for a time.

The pier grew more crowded as day tourists arrived, making their way from other islands to sample the small Key's quieter attractions.

''Do you still dive?'' Roman asked when the bucket finally emptied.

Still? Her expression must have revealed her confusion.

"I thought you said you enjoyed diving," he explained.

"No, no, I didn't. I don't dive. I have a phobia about the water, actually."

He watched her for a strange beat. She was very aware of how close he stood to her, of the strangers walking past, of the sun hitting his strong arms and the warm scent of him pulling her and pushing her away all at once.

"You live on an island that's two miles wide and you're afraid of the water?"

"Yep. Well, I don't mind looking at it. I just—I don't go into it."

"Do you know why you're afraid?"

She shook her head. He picked up the bucket and they began walking back toward the marina.

"I believe in facing your fears," he said. "Head-on."

"You don't want to see me have a panic attack," she told him. "It's not a pretty sight."

He stopped short.

"You have panic attacks?" Concern etched a new line across his forehead.

"I'm making a great impression on my potential new boss, aren't I? I'm freaked out about dating, I'm afraid of water, I have panic attacks. I swear, I'm perfectly fine at the bar. I don't crack up in front of customers. Much." She looked at him. "That was a joke," she added.

"I don't think you're nuts," he said. He cocked his head, regarded her for a beat. "I think you're everything Morrie said you were."

She wondered exactly what Morrie had told him.

They reached the marina and he returned the bucket. There was a sink for hand-washing, and after they finished, he held the door open for her again. Great. He was gorgeous, rich, nice *and* polite. She needed to find some faults, quickly. She reminded herself that she barely knew him and had no reason to trust him. She brushed by him, back into the harsh glare of the day.

"I need to get back to the bar," she said.

"I thought you didn't have to be back till later."

No, damn him. "I could show you the books." Anything to cut short their outing. "You don't want to spend too much time in the sun right away," she added, trying to think of more reasons they should go back to the bar. "I'm used to it, but you're not. The sun here is seductive. It's stronger than you think. You can tell the tourists because they're the ones who are sunburned. And by the way, don't swim after dark. That's when the sharks are most active. The mosquitoes here are ferocious, too. And you need some sunglasses—the kind that protect against ultraviolet rays—"

She stopped. He was watching her with his curiously level gaze shuttered and hard to read now. But he could read *her,* apparently. And she hated that. It made her heart thump and pound, and she wanted to run, hard, fast, until she couldn't think or feel.

"I didn't want to make you uncomfortable," he said. "Or take up too much of your time. Let's go back."

All he did was make her feel uncomfortable. But now she felt like a jerk.

"No, I'll walk you into the town. Morrie asked me to do anything for you that I could, and I owe him…everything. If you'd like me to show you around some more—''

''And take me shopping for sunglasses?'' The teasing note returned to his voice.

She felt her cheeks heat. ''I really wasn't trying to ditch you,'' she lied.

He didn't believe her, she suspected, but he didn't confront her about it, either.

''Good thing,'' he said. ''Because I'm not going anywhere. I'm here to stay.''

That was exactly what she was afraid of.

Chapter 4

He wanted to move a hell of a lot faster, but she wasn't ready.

Roman sat in Morrie's office, the bar's account books spread out around him, pretending to give a rat's ass if the bar was making money or not. All he really cared about was why Leah was so scared—not just of him, but of everything. *She was scared of the water.* That had blown his mind. Leah loved to swim. She'd been the one who'd insisted he take diving lessons, get the required certification before they'd come to Thunder Key. She'd been fearless. They'd explored the coral channels and canyons together, snorkeled and bodysurfed and played like kids in the calm waters of the barrier-reef-protected shore. She'd made *him*— stuffed shirt that he'd been—play, too.

Now she was afraid of the very thing she'd loved most. Water. Did it go back to the accident? That had to have been harrowing, her car going over the bridge that way. He couldn't even imagine. Hell, he didn't want to, but he couldn't stop. What had really happened to her? It wasn't just water that she feared, and that made him wonder if something worse than he had ever imagined had occurred on that fateful night. It was as if she feared life itself. She held back. His Leah had never held back.

He was going to have to go easy with her, and that would be the hardest thing he'd ever done in his life. He wanted to charge in, take control. That was what he'd been born and raised to do in every aspect of his life. But that had never worked with Leah.

They'd gone ahead and walked into the town before coming back to the bar. Thunder Key the town was like a miniature New England village, with twisty palm-shrouded lanes and predominantly shotgun-style wooden houses mixed in with other styles, most with the unifying gingerbread trim that formed the backbone of the Keysy conch architecture. Leah kept up a steady stream of information as they walked. There were bike rental shops and art galleries alongside little bars and restaurants that clearly catered to the tourist crowd.

"The Shark and Fin is more a local thing," she'd said. "Morrie liked it that way. Of course, you could really beef up the business if you wanted to do a little advertising."

"I want to keep the Shark and Fin just the way it is," he'd reiterated. "If making a million bucks a year was all I cared about anymore, I'd have stayed in New York."

That was as personal as the conversation had gotten.

Roman shut the books. The bar did a good business. The bills were paid up-to-date, and the staff didn't appear to have much turnover. He didn't want to rush into the deal, though. What if Leah left Thunder Key? He had no guarantee she'd stay on after he bought it. For now he got the sense she felt an obligation to Morrie to watch over the bar while he was trying to sell it.

No way was Roman rushing this deal.

Morrie wasn't in a hurry, either. It was clear he was concerned about who bought the bar and what would happen afterward. In particular, he was worried about Leah. Morrie had carefully avoided giving any personal information about Leah to Roman, but the older man clearly respected and cared deeply about the woman he'd left in charge of his bar. Smart, hard-working, reliable…the list of compliments for Leah had gone on and on. And glad as he was that there had been a kind, caring person to watch over Leah when she'd needed it, it still bugged the hell out of him that it had been a stranger.

Why hadn't Leah come to *him?* She'd lost her memory, yet run to Thunder Key. Why?

It drove him insane to think about it. There was a place in his heart that wanted to believe she'd come here instinctively, drawn by the happy moments they'd spent on Thunder Key together.

But she'd still blocked *him* out. She'd come to Thunder Key, not to Roman.

The office phone rang but he didn't pick up. It was connected to the same line that was in the bar, and he had no reason to expect a call. Then Joey stuck his head in the door and told him the phone was for him.

He should have known.

"Hey, bud."

"Mark." He should have known his mother would get right on the question of what Roman was doing giving up all readily accessible means of communication and buying a bar in the Keys. And since his parents and sister had made no headway with him, she'd turned to his brother-in-law to do the job.

"So it's true. You're buying a bar in the Keys."

"Yes. I'm buying a bar in the Keys," Roman said mechanically. "Anything else I can help you with, Mark? I'm pretty busy here, actually."

"Just checking on you. There are people who care about you, you know. And we worry."

Yes, he knew. "I appreciate that, Mark. But you can tell everyone that I'm not ready for the straitjacket yet. I'm making an investment. That's all. Just doing business."

"I hope that's all it is," Mark said. He hesitated a beat. "Roman, those questions you were asking me the other day, about amnesia…"

Roman tensed. "What about it?"

"Why were you asking those questions?"

"I don't have time to talk, Mark."

"Roman, I know sometimes when people are going through the grief process, there's a part of them that wants to look in every face and see the person they've lost. They never found Leah's body and that was hard for you to deal with. But she's dead. There's no way she could have survived. If you think you're going to find her again in Thunder Key, if you've got some crazy scenario going in your head that she survived

the crash and is living in Thunder Key with amnesia—''

Roman closed his eyes for a frustrated beat. His
blood pressure was fast approaching the danger point.

''There's no point wallowing in that girl's death,''
Mark said. ''I'm sorry that she died. We're all sorry
that she died. But you've got to move on now. I hate
to say it, but you're better off without her and—''

That did it.

''I'm not better off without her. In fact, I'm not
planning to be without her!'' Damn. He hadn't meant
to blurt that out. Seeing Leah again had sent his emotional control into a tailspin.

''That sounds crazy, Roman. That's what she did to
you. She made you crazy. You weren't yourself after
you married her.''

''No, I *was* myself after I married her and that was
the whole problem.''

''The problem was you married the wrong woman.
And she died. It was tragic, but it's over. You need
help, Roman. You need—''

''I need Leah. And I don't give a damn how you
or anyone else feels about it. I'm not crazy. She's here,
Mark. She's alive.'' God, he hadn't meant to tell him
that. He wanted to bang the phone down in frustration,
but he couldn't leave it this way. ''I don't know what
happened the night her car went over that bridge, but
I'm going to find out. And you're going to stay the
hell out of it.''

''Roman—''

''Don't say a word about this to Gen or my parents.
You know how they are, how they felt about Leah.
About our marriage. And with everything I'm trying

to work through now... They don't need to know. Not right now. It would just upset them, and you know it. And do not—I repeat, do not—come down to the Keys. Don't even call again. Tell my family I'm fine— because that's the truth, and that's all they need to know.'' He took another steadying breath. He had to get Mark on his side. ''Mark, I know you love Gen. Think how you'd feel if she disappeared and then you found her again. I need time. I'm counting on you to give me that.''

Mark was silent for a beat. ''All right. I won't tell anyone about Leah—if that's really who it is. You're right—that information would just upset people. But be careful. And I mean that.''

Roman hung up the phone and headed straight for the kitchen, drawn by the smell of frying fish and the hope that Leah was there. He had to see her again. Telling someone she was alive had felt so strange. No doubt Mark thought he was nuts now. Sometimes even *he* thought he was nuts. Every time Leah was out of his sight, he started to think he'd imagined her all over again.

Could he trust Mark to keep the news about Leah quiet? The truth was, he didn't know. But there'd be hell to pay if anyone in his family interfered with him and Leah now.

Joey was at the stove, ladling chowder into a huge bowl.

''Leah said to help yourself,'' Joey said. ''If you're thinking about buying the bar, you might as well find out if you like my cooking.''

''Does Leah cook?'' She'd been the worst cook in the world, which he'd always found oddly charming since she was so creative in other ways. To find her running a bar and grill was ironic.

"Nope. She has a black thumb in the kitchen, she says." Joey watched him. "Are you really interested in the bar, or are you just trying to hook up with Leah?"

"Well, why don't you tell me what's really on your mind," Roman said dryly.

Joey didn't smile. "We're shorthanded today. One of the waitresses called in sick. Want to help out?"

Roman figured that was as much leeway as he was going to get from the wary cook. "All right." In New York he sat behind a desk and ran the show. In the Keys he was just another guy, even if he was possibly Joey's new boss. He'd have to prove himself. It surprised him that he didn't mind. In fact, he took it as a challenge. "Where's this going?" He took the bowl of chowder. Joey ladled out a second one.

The cook pointed to a numbered table layout, faded and splattered, nailed on the wall. "Table six." He turned back to the stove.

Roman carried the bowls out through the swinging doors that separated the kitchen from the bar. The phone was ringing behind the bar. Leah finished filling a glass at the beer tap, then picked it up.

"Shark and Fin."

Roman moved through the bar, set the bowls of chowder in front of the men at table six. When he turned back to the bar, Leah had an irritated frown on her face. She hung up the phone.

"You're waiting tables now?" she asked.

"Sure. Might as well get to know the business from the ground up. I'm thorough. That's how I operate."

She went back to the beer tap, filled another glass. "Great," she said, pushing a tray at him. She put a couple more beers on it. "That goes to the table by the door."

And for the next hour and a half, Roman wore his feet out going back and forth between the kitchen and the bar and the various tables. He noticed that Leah kept up a relaxed interchange with the customers, whose garb varied between scruffy fishermen's duds and T-shirts and shorts. She smiled that crooked, killer smile of hers—but never at Roman. Whenever he caught her eye, her expression would immediately darken, something frightened lurking there.

He tried to think of ways to approach her without scaring her, but couldn't think of a damn one except for the one he couldn't possibly do, which involved kissing the hell out of her. It just about turned his torn-up heart inside out every time he looked at her. Not being able to touch her—yet seeing her, being so close to her—was worse than any medieval torture.

The lunch crowd thinned, and Joey had the temerity to put him to work doing dishes. Roman was pretty sure the cook was testing him. He took it as another challenge and loaded and unloaded every plate as if he was making a fortune on Wall Street doing it.

By the time he was nearly done, his hands were red from the hot water. He hadn't seen Leah in way too long. He was like an addict, but he had no intention of getting Leah out of his system.

He was on the last load when he heard the sound of the swinging door.

"Whoa," he said, turning his head to see her stop

short as she almost ran into him in the cramped space. She had a tray full of beer mugs in her hands.

He could hear the phone ringing from the now-quiet bar. The jukebox had been going all through lunch, but the bar had emptied for the afternoon lull.

"Wow, now you're doing dishes. You're really serious about this."

"Morrie suggested I get a little hands-on experience," Roman explained. The small washer in the narrow galley-style kitchen was only a few feet from the door. Leah stood there with the tray, looking as if she wanted to just turn around and back out, and dammit, he didn't want her to.

He picked up a dish, trying to think of something to say to make her stay.

"So," he started gamely, turning back to look at her over his shoulder as he placed the dish into the washer rack. "When does it usually pick up—"

"Leah—" Joey called her name as he pushed through the swinging doors. Leah started to move out of the way but lost her balance, the tray of mugs teetering in her hands.

Roman had just enough time to turn and grab her.

The tray of mugs—some empty, some not—went flying as Leah stumbled forward. Straight into Roman. He couldn't have been holding her any closer if he'd tried. He managed to catch her before she hit the floor—but not before she wound up wet. Shattered mugs lay everywhere as the odor of spilled beer filled the air.

Leah caught herself by grabbing on to him, too. For just a second, an incredible heartbeat, her green sea-storm eyes flashed at his and she was in his arms. His heart went nuts. He wasn't thinking, just reacting, and he pulled her against him, closed his eyes, breathed.

Breathed Leah.

"Oh, God, I'm sorry." Joey's voice broke through the moment.

Leah untangled herself from Roman's arms.

The sudden feeling of bereavement shocked him. For that one second, he'd held Leah. He'd had no idea how wonderful…and how awful…it would be.

Because now she wouldn't even look at him. It was as if he was the bubonic plague, personified.

"I'm okay," she said. "Just wet, that's all." She gave a little laugh, but it sounded forced. "What a mess."

"I'll get it," Roman said. "You might want to get changed."

Her damp shirt clung to her softly rounded breasts. She went for a broom and dustpan.

"Leah, the phone was for you," Joey said.

Roman took the broom out of her hand. "I'll take care of this."

"Thank you." Still, she didn't look at him. "Who's on the phone?" she asked Joey.

"I don't know. Someone asking for you," Joey said with a shrug.

Leah disappeared through the swinging doors.

Roman finished up, then went out into the bar. Leah stood behind the bar counter, staring at the phone.

"Everything okay?" he asked.

She nodded. "Fine." She gave him a quick look, then crossed her arms over the front of her wet shirt, now plastered to her breasts. "I've got to change.

Don't want the customers thinking we're running a wet T-shirt contest.''

"Wait!"

She chewed her lip, turned back.

"I'm sorry about getting you wet. I couldn't catch you and the tray—"

"Not your fault. Thanks for cleaning up the mess."

He hesitated. "How about I rustle up some leftovers, whatever I can come up with in the kitchen, and we have a late lunch in Morrie's office. I've got a couple questions."

He didn't have any questions, but he'd make some up if he had to. "You do eat, right? I promise, I don't bite. Hard."

She laughed, and this time she met his eyes. "Okay. Thanks."

Progress, Roman thought. Tiny steps.

He wanted to take flying leaps, but he'd be satisfied with one tiny step at a time. For now.

Leah ran up the back stairs. She felt off, weird. She didn't know if it was because she'd literally fallen into Roman's arms—and he'd been muscle, all muscle— or because that was twice now that someone had hung up on her on the phone.

It creeped her out, being hung up on. Twice. The first time, it was probably just a wrong number. It wasn't uncommon for someone to mistakenly call the Shark and Fin, thinking they'd dialed their aunt's or cousin's or best friend's number instead. But the second time, someone had asked Joey for Leah. Then they'd hung up. It was probably nothing, but it bothered her just the same. Anything out of the norm bothered her.

Roman bothered her.

But how could she say no to lunch? It was an innocuous request. He was interested in the bar. There
was no solid reason to think he wasn't legit.

Morrie was going to check him out. She wondered
if he'd found out anything.

When she reached her apartment, she shut the door
and peeled off her wet shirt. Her body felt chilled even
in the warm lazy air of her apartment. Quickly she
tried to wipe the beer smell from her with a damp
cloth, then she pulled on another T-shirt from a
drawer. It was hot pink, like her nails. It had the number thirteen on the front.

She liked the number thirteen. She had no idea why,
as usual. But she'd been drawn to the shirt the second
she'd laid eyes on it in the T-shirt shop in Smugglers
Village.

Just like she was drawn to Roman.

But something bothered her about Roman, too, and
she was too confused to figure out whether it was that
she was attracted to him or that he was someone from
the past. Maybe he reminded her of someone from the
past. He'd said they didn't know each other. But trusting him was no easy thing. She barely knew him.

She took the phone from the little kitchenette and
curled up on the love seat.

"Hey, Morrie," she said when he picked up.

"How's my girl?"

"Good." Just hearing Morrie's voice soothed her
nerves. She missed him, missed his stabilizing presence in her life. But she had to get used to his being

gone. If the bar sold, that would be it. He'd move to New Mexico. She couldn't depend on Morrie forever. "I just wanted to let you know how things were going." She just wanted to hear his fatherly voice.

She told him about her tour of the town with Roman, how he'd helped out around the bar.

"We're about to go to your office to talk about the books. I wanted to let you know, to see if you'd be available if he has any questions I can't answer."

"I'll be here," Morrie said. "I put in a couple calls to New York. Bradshaw's a pretty well-known name there. Roman Bradshaw is one of the heirs to the zillion-dollar Bradshaw dynasty. His family owns Bradshaw Securities, among other things. It's some kind of Wall Street trading firm. He's got money running through his veins. Apparently his wife died a while back and he's taken a leave from the company."

Leah's grip on the phone tightened. She didn't know if she was relieved, or even more worried. Roman was for real. Great. He wasn't some kind of weirdo trying to make a play for her and using the bar as an excuse. It was also true that he had a recently deceased wife. But this meant he really did have the money to buy the bar. He'd be part of her life, unless she left. That was an option she'd never considered and didn't want to consider now.

Thunder Key was the only home she knew.

Get over it, Leah. He's just a man.

Just a hot, intense, heart-stoppingly gorgeous man who had the saddest eyes she'd ever seen…and the cutest smile. All at once.

Morrie promised he'd be around if she needed to

call with questions, and she uncurled from the love seat. Time to go down to the office.

She darted a quick look in the mirror in her bathroom. She ran a comb through her hair and started to pick up a tube of lipstick, then stopped.

What was she doing? This was *not* a date.

She headed down the stairs. Roman waited for her in Morrie's office. He had two plates of Joey's fish and chips laid out on the desk. Napkins. A bottle of beer for each of them. He'd even brought ketchup and tartar sauce.

"Thanks." She sat down.

He'd pulled up a folding chair from somewhere and left Morrie's creaky but comfortable desk chair for her. Of course, she wasn't comfortable. Not with Roman Bradshaw sitting next to her, with his midnight-ocean eyes and too-nice smile.

"Dig in," he said when she didn't start eating right away.

She dipped a bite of fish in the tartar sauce, then in the ketchup, the way she liked it. When she looked up, Roman was watching her. His eyes were nice, if a little haunted, and the look he was giving her was appreciative without being leering. It was an oddly serious look, as if he were truly looking not *at* her but *inside* her.

"If you keep looking at me like that, I'll never be able to eat," she said. "And I'm hungry. So stop it already."

He blinked, as if she'd roused him from some faraway place he'd gone for a second. "I'm sorry. I was just thinking—"

"What?" She stuck the bite in her mouth, chewed.

Joey's deep-fried fish was the best on Thunder Key, which was why the locals flocked to the Shark and Fin.

"I was just wondering if you're from around here," he said.

"I've lived here as long as I can remember," she answered. Which was actually true. So there. She hated lying to people, which was one of the reasons she avoided getting close to anyone. If Roman Bradshaw didn't think she was nuts already, he would when he found out she'd lost her memory. And wasn't doing a damn thing about getting it back because the whole idea freaked her out every time she thought about it.

She was definitely screwed up. It wasn't a little factoid about herself that she enjoyed sharing with just anyone.

"What about you?" she asked to turn the tables.

"I grew up in Manhattan." He took a swallow of beer, put the bottle down. "All my life. My family runs a financial company."

He said it as if it were no big deal, which of course now that she'd spoken with Morrie, she knew it was. The zillion-dollar Bradshaw dynasty, that's how Morrie had put it. *Money running through his veins.*

Even wearing his only-slightly damp T-shirt and lean, mean jeans, Roman Bradshaw would never look like a regular guy. He was just too clean-cut, sharp, rich looking. He exuded power and wealth.

He dug into the fish and chips.

"So what do they think about you leaving the family business?"

"Not happy," he said between bites.

"Maybe you'll change your mind. Go back." It just seemed too weird that he could leave his whole life behind. Especially since, unlike her, he could remember *his* life.

"I don't think so." He looked her square in the eyes again. "My old life— That was someone else. Not me. Not anymore. I don't even want to know that guy. He was a bastard. All he cared about was work and money. His priorities were all screwed up."

Damn. This was getting personal again. And getting personal about Roman Bradshaw was as dangerous as getting personal about herself.

He stirred a finger of fried fish around in his ketchup.

"My wife, she wanted me to slow down. Relax. Smell the roses. I completely ignored her." He took a bite of the fish.

Well, if Leah still thought he was trying to court her, this conversation sealed it that he wasn't. He certainly wasn't trying to impress her. Not when he kept telling her what an ass he'd been all his life. But actually, she was impressed. Roman had a way of facing himself that she envied.

She was way too scared to face too many things about her own life.

"It's hard to lose someone you love," she said softly. It was obvious he was carrying a big load of guilt on his shoulders.

"Have you ever lost someone you loved?" His voice was quiet, but his gaze was intense in that way he had of making her feel as if he could peer right into her skull.

She took a sip of her beer.

"No, I haven't," she said finally, and she watched as something dark entered his eyes. She chose her words carefully. "I just…was imagining how it would feel, I guess."

He looked away. "You're lucky."

"You think about your wife a lot." It wasn't a question. It was clear he thought full-time about the woman he'd lost.

"Every minute." Still no eye contact. "At first, I thought it was something you just got over. Like a broken bone. But it's not." He looked her straight in the eyes now. And the pain she saw there just about broke her own heart. "You don't get over losing someone. Particularly when it was your own fault. But you can change. And that's what I'm determined to do. I learned a lot—about myself, about her, about what really matters in life. And I have no idea why I'm laying all this on you. We just met yesterday. You probably don't want to hear all my weird head stuff."

"No, it's okay." Had she actually said that? But she couldn't stand how hard he was on himself, and she sensed he didn't talk about his wife to just anyone. He was reserved, and yet he kept opening up to her. Maybe it was being on Thunder Key, or maybe it was just because she was a woman who'd made it clear friendship was all she had to offer. But the evident pain within Roman Bradshaw was impossible to ignore. "Hey, I have weird head stuff, too. I think I already made that pretty plain."

He laughed. "That's right. We have something in common."

She smiled back at him. Damn those dimples of his. "You know," she said, serious again, "you probably should see a grief counselor or something. I mean, I'm saying that as a friend.'' And as a hypocrite, of course, since she'd refused to see a doctor about her own problems.

He was shaking his head. ''I'm all right. What I need is Thunder Key.''

''There *is* something healing about the Keys,'' she had to agree. ''Sun, sand, sea, freedom. No shoes, no past, no problems.''

He was looking at her oddly, but he didn't ask what she meant. She was relieved.

''You know, it never freezes here,'' she said to defuse the strange moment. ''And the sun shines almost every day of the year. That's why they call it paradise. Even when it rains in Miami, it's dry here. Key West is the driest city in Florida. If it weren't for hurricanes, the Keys would be perfect.''

Back to the weather. A safe topic.

Roman seemed to take the cue. He opened Morrie's account books. He asked questions as they continued eating, and she gave him answers. She was sure the Shark and Fin was a piece of cake compared to the business he was accustomed to helming, but Roman was a thorough guy, as he'd said. He didn't miss a thing.

Scary, that.

The phone rang and she picked up.

''Hello, Shark and Fin.''

There was silence on the line, then— ''I know who you are. I know what you've done.''

She didn't even feel the phone drop out of her hand.

Chapter 5

Her face turned completely white. The phone hit the wood floor with a thud. Roman thought for a second she was going to faint, but what happened was worse.

He'd never seen anyone have a panic attack before.

"Leah, what happened?" He reached for her hand. Her fingers were cold, shaking, and yet he saw sweat popping out on her brow.

She grabbed her hand away, pressed both hands to her stomach.

"Oh, God, I'm going to be sick," she whispered, and then covered her mouth with one palm, twisted out of her seat, banging Morrie's chair against the office wall.

She rushed from the room, her eyes wild. Roman chased up the stairs after her. She tore open the door of her apartment. One part of him wanted to go back down to the office, find out who was on the phone, figure out what the hell was going on, but no way was he leaving Leah alone.

He found her leaning over the commode.

"Go away," she cried roughly.

"Not going anywhere." He couldn't see her face. She wouldn't look at him. One hand was still on her mouth, and she just hunched there, trembling. He wanted to go to her, hold her, but he knew she wouldn't want that. He felt helpless and he hated it. "Who was on the phone?"

"Nobody. I don't know."

"Then what—"

"I'm telling you, I don't know." Leah's head reeled. Had that voice been real? Or her imagination? God, she was freaked out from the two hang-ups earlier, and maybe she'd just thought she'd heard a voice say those words. Words she'd heard in her nightmares. And now she was out of control, in her bathroom, with Roman Bradshaw.

Her every nerve ending tingled. Tremors possessed her. She couldn't think straight to save her life. Racing heartbeat. Fear of...dying. The whole range of horror washed over her. It made no sense, never did. Panic attacks were hell and she hated them. It pissed her off that she couldn't control them.

"I'm all right," she said. Thank God she hadn't vomited. There was one small favor. "Leave me alone." *Please.*

"No, no, you're not okay. I don't know what happened, but I'm not leaving you alone."

His voice was so comforting. If he took her in his arms right this minute, she'd lay her head back on his big shoulder and cry. But—no way was she doing that. She blinked fast, a couple of times.

Deep breaths, deep breaths.

"I'm really not going to explode or anything," she joked. "It's no biggie. Just a minor meltdown."

"Can I do anything, get you anything?"

She shook her head. "I think I'm okay now," she said after another minute. "I'm not going to be sick. Yay me." She tried a half laugh. Take that, panic attack. She'd beaten it. For now.

He helped her up. Her knees felt like Jell-O that wasn't ready yet.

"Come on." He led her out to the love seat. She watched as he went into the kitchenette and found where she kept the glasses. He filled one up with water. "Drink."

She took a sip. It was hard swallowing past the lump in her throat. The panic attacks always made her feel as if she were choking.

"How long have you been experiencing panic attacks?" he asked.

"A while." She set the glass down. Her hand barely shook. "It's a little embarrassing. Actually, a lot embarrassing."

He sat down beside her. Not close enough to be touching, but almost. She avoided his laser gaze by staring at his jean-clad legs. He had very long legs.

"Thanks for...being there," she said. "Just for future reference, hanging out with me when I'm throwing up is above and beyond the call of duty." She tried to laugh again, but it came out a little bit like a sob. She bit her lip and swallowed hard over the lump in her throat.

She was surprised when she felt the warm tip of his fingers touch her chin, drawing her gaze up to meet his.

"Hey, don't be embarrassed. I'm just worried about you. What happened down there?" He watched her, a furrow creasing his brow. He wasn't touching her anymore, but he was still close. Way too close.

She scooted a bit more into the corner of the love seat, shook her head. "Nothing. It's just…one of those stupid panic attack things. Something gets in my head, and then all of a sudden every time the phone rings, I'm out of control. There were a couple hang-ups earlier, and now the phone is freaking me out."

"Hang-ups? Just today, or before?"

"Just today. Probably wrong numbers."

"Joey said someone asked for you," he pointed out. "Was that one of the hang-ups?"

"Probably just a disconnection."

"What else prompts your panic attacks? I don't really know much about panic attacks."

He seemed truly interested, but she felt strange having this discussion.

"Anything." She shrugged. "It doesn't have to make sense, so if you're looking for it to fit into some reasonable explanation, it's not going to happen. Panic attacks defy logic." She'd read up on anxiety in the small library at Thunder Key. There were certain medications that helped alleviate the symptoms in some people, but she knew that wasn't the answer to her problem. There was something inside her head, in her memories. Something dark and frightening that came to her in bits and pieces and nightmares.

She didn't want to know.

"I really can't talk about this," she told him.

"Maybe you need to," he pressed gently, his eyes somber.

"You must be a sucker for punishment if you want to hear more about my problems," she teased, trying to put the conversation on a lighter track. But the sadness remained in his eyes.

"I've just figured out that holding something in doesn't make it go away, that's all," he said. "That's what I tried to do when my wife died. Hold it all in. I was afraid to deal with it."

He got up, walked to the window. Pushing back the sheers, he stared out at the sea.

"How did she die?" Leah asked softly. "You mentioned it was an accident."

"Car accident." He stood very still. "Her car went into a river." His voice was low, pained. "They thought—they told me she drowned. I can't even imagine what she must have gone through that night. It had to have been terrifying."

Leah didn't think, just stood up, moved toward him. He looked so alone, silhouetted against the bright day outside.

"It was unreal. The search went on for days. Her car wasn't found right away."

Oh, God. How had Roman survived that kind of misery? Just the thought of someone being trapped underwater made Leah feel sick again.

"I couldn't believe it was true. I was sure they'd find her, alive. I hoped they'd find her alive. I didn't want to give up hope. But then…there was no more hope."

"They found her body?"

Days. Days of waiting for them to find his wife's body, to drag it out of a river.

He turned, and his unwavering gaze met hers. He was silent for a terrible moment.

"No."

Leah's eyes filled. It was killing Roman not to put his arms around her and say, But I've found you now.

There was no way he could do that.

"It was the hardest thing I've ever had to accept in my life," he went on. "That she wasn't found. That I wasn't with her. That I didn't do something, anything, different."

"Roman," she whispered. Then her hand was on his, her soft fingers twining between his. "If you'd been with her, you might have died, too."

He'd thought of that. Plenty of times. And there'd been plenty of times he'd wished he had been in that car, that he had gone over that bridge with her.

Until he'd come to Thunder Key again.

"The hardest thing to live with is regret," he said quietly.

She watched him, her eyes still shiny, wet, hurting for him. It was so painful not to pull her closer.

He settled for squeezing her hand. "Every day is precious, important, maybe the last one you'll have." He shook his head. "Now I sound like a greeting card or something," he cracked.

She smiled, which was what he'd been hoping she'd do.

"I think you sound like a smart guy," she said. She gave his hand a squeeze now. "Pretty inspiring, actually. Your wife was lucky to have you, whether you know it or not."

It was surreal, having this conversation with Leah. It hurt too much to go on with it. There were still too many things unsaid, but now they were things he had no choice about, despite his impatience.

Slow, slow, slow. It was so hard to take things slow.

The phone rang. She startled, her eyes flashing up at him, then away.

"Do you want me—"

"No." She crossed the room, picked up the phone. "Morrie." She sounded relieved. "Hi. Yes, everything's fine." The conversation went on. Roman watched her for a long beat, then looked away, feeling stupidly jealous of the bar owner who could make Leah relax in an instant of hearing his voice.

She finished the call.

"Well, while you're feeling inspired," he said, turning back to her as she walked toward him, "how would you feel about a little walk on the beach? It'd do you good not to hear a phone ringing for a while, and the bar won't get busy again for a bit."

He wanted her all to himself.

She hesitated.

He added, "You know it's National Take a City Boy to the Beach Day, don't you? I'm sure you want to participate." It was something Leah used to do all the time—just make up holidays. Any time he didn't want to do something, she'd claim it was a national holiday.

She smiled, a little nervously, but a smile just the same. "Okay. It would be good to get out of the bar for a little bit, anyway. You're right, I really don't need to hear the phone ring."

They walked downstairs, into the heat of the day.

The beach outside the Shark and Fin was quiet, the water hypnotically smooth. They took their shoes off at the end of the wooden sidewalk that led off from the bar's outside deck.

The sand felt hot and grainy beneath his feet. He wanted to take her hand, but he restrained himself. They walked by the shore. A boat sailed along in the distance.

"So what about people who don't live near the water?" she said idly. "What do they do on National Take a City Boy to the Beach Day?"

He noticed she was staring out at the blue sea as they walked, not at him. What was she thinking? He'd give anything to know.

"They're just out of luck," he said. "Damn, you're lucky."

She looked at him then, and her eyes sparkled in the bright sun. She laughed.

He was the lucky one. He'd never felt luckier, ever. They walked for a while, talking lazily. Nothing personal. There was an abandoned lighthouse nearby, and she took him inside. From there they could see over the trees to the rooftops of the town, its crisscrossing streets forming a visual crazy quilt.

"This isn't the original lighthouse," she told him. "The first one was swept out to sea by a hurricane. Several people died who'd sheltered inside." Her expression looked serious, and she stared out at the sea. "I think about them being trapped—"

Roman watched her. Leah had been trapped, inside her car. In that river. Did she remember anything about it? She'd admitted her fear of water. But when he told her about his wife's death in a car accident—a drowning—she hadn't seemed to feel anything but sympathy for him.

"Sometimes, I dream about being trapped underwater," she said softly, so softly he had to lean in to hear her.

He waited, wondering—

But then she shook her head. "Let's go."

If she had any memories, she wasn't sharing them with him.

They climbed down from the top of the lighthouse and walked back toward the Shark and Fin. The afternoon was hot, but a soft breeze played across the sea.

"Do you have any kids?" she asked suddenly, as if she'd just thought of the possibility. "I was just, you know, wondering about when you move here—"

"Nope. No kids. My wife wanted kids. Right away. I said no, of course."

"Why of course?"

He gave her a look.

"I mean, besides the fact that you were a bastard. You've established that," she said teasingly, gently.

"I didn't think I'd be a good father," he told her. "That's the real reason. I told her a bunch of lies— about how I wasn't ready yet. I wanted to get more established. I had a whole plan for my life, and kids didn't fit in until I'd accomplished certain goals."

"And that wasn't true?"

They'd stopped near the shore. The water was only a few feet away. He took her hand, tugged her down, and they sat on the soft-packed pebbly sand. His jeans were going to be covered in sand, but he didn't care.

"Great big pile of garbage," he said quietly. "I

would love to have kids. She would be—would have been—a great mom.''

"You know, not to be disrespectful or anything, but I'm sure she wasn't perfect," Leah said, her eyes soft on him.

"She was pushy," he said. "But that was actually endearing. She was always trying to get me to do crazy things."

"I bet she thought you were endearing, too. You're a nice guy, Roman Bradshaw."

He liked the way the sun lit up her eyes. He was still holding her hand, and for just a beat, it felt real. This closeness.

But she didn't know him, not really. She had blocked him completely from her mind.

"Well, you're seeing Roman Bradshaw Version 2.0," he pointed out. "This is the advanced model."

Ah, that crooked, heart-killing smile of hers came out to play then. Would she still smile when she knew the whole truth? How could he convince her that he had changed when in the process he was still lying to her, if only by omission? What other choice did he have?

The more time he spent with her, the harder it became to hold back the truth. And the angrier she might be when she finally learned it.

"So why didn't you think you'd be a good dad?"

He took his hand from hers. Sharing his feelings was a new thing and he still struggled with it. Especially with Leah, because he had to be so careful with his words. Slowly he drew a line in the moist sand in front of them. The water lapped softly at the shore a foot away from where they sat.

''I wanted to be a different kind of father than my father was to me. But— I don't know how, I guess,'' he admitted. ''My family is…distant. Very reserved. Most of us spend almost twenty-four/seven together at the firm. And yet I don't know them at all. They're strangers. That's how my family operates. Emotions are to be kept under wraps. We're all business, all the time. She wasn't like that.''

''What was she like? Tell me something about her.''

Her expression was pained, and it took him a second to realize she was hurting for *him*.

''She was carefree. She didn't like making plans. She would just do whatever came to mind. She drove me nuts because I needed plans, schedules, for everything.'' That was the Leah she used to be when fear didn't lurk in the shadows of her green eyes. ''I like to feel in control, and she made me feel out of control.'' She still made him feel out of control. He still didn't know how to deal with her.

He leaned forward, dipped his finger in the warm water. Sitting back, he took her hand, turned it over and placed the wet tip of his finger inside her palm, then folded her fingers over it.

Her eyes locked with his, connecting, holding. She didn't move away.

''Feel that?'' he said quietly. ''It's the sea.''

She nodded.

He forced himself to move his hand away.

''Scared?''

''No. Yes. I don't know.''

She looked oddly confused now, and he wanted to just put his arms around her and tell her everything was going to be all right. But he still wasn't sure about that himself. The future was a blank slate.

"It's time to go back," she said. She stood, brushed the back of her pants, then stopped, her attention seeming caught by something up the beach. "There's a turtle."

Roman turned, following her gaze.

"Oh, look, there's something wrong with it," she whispered, and started running.

Roman caught up to her as she knelt down on the wet sand at the sea's edge. Leah's eyes narrowed critically on the hard-shelled reptile limping along the beach in front of her, and only when Roman reached her did he see what she saw—a piece of fishing wire wrapped around a front flipper.

He looked at Leah, not surprised at all by the sudden anger in her eyes. It was like Leah to feel immediate empathy for any creature. What did surprise him was the tightness banding his chest. Then he realized why. This was *his* Leah. She'd changed in so many ways, but the familiarity of her reaction to the wounded turtle hit him hard. He knew she'd want to do something. She'd want to save it. That was Leah.

"Why's it tagged?" he asked, seeing a small red band on one of the turtle's uninjured rear flippers.

"It's been to the turtle hospital." Leah reached out, touched the turtle's back, stopping it in its uneven track. "And it needs to go back. I hope I can pick it up."

"We will," he said determinedly.

Leah looked up at him, seeming startled as her mouth parted. "You're going to help me?"

"Where's the turtle hospital?"

"Orchid Key." She looked wary still, as if she didn't expect—or want—his assistance. She seemed to search his face for— What? He had no idea.

"Let's go."

She was right, the thing was heavy. Roman spanned his hands across the back of the turtle, curling around its side. It hobbled backward, flapping its flippers in protest. His arms brushed Leah's as they lifted it. She jerked back and they almost dropped the turtle.

Roman stared at her, seeing the brief glimmer of fear in her eyes. God, was she afraid of him still? Then the look was gone, hidden behind a mask of concern directed solely at the turtle. It had happened so fast, he wasn't sure if he'd seen it. He only knew he hated it, whatever it was.

He wanted her to trust him. But he was going to have to earn her trust, and that was going to take time. He was impatient. He wanted her to trust him *now,* and dammit, she didn't.

They made it to the Shark and Fin. Leah nodded toward a beat-up truck in the parking lot. "That's Morrie's. He left me the keys to use it if I need it. Wait here. I'll be right back."

She ran inside, leaving Roman holding the turtle on the pavement. This was, he thought to himself wryly, a typical Leah episode. One minute you're taking a walk on the beach, the next you're on your way to a turtle hospital.

He didn't realize he was smiling until she burst back out of the bar with the keys.

She stopped short.

"What?" he asked in response to her baffled expression.

She shook her head. "I don't know. You're just—looking at me weird. Smiling at me like—" She didn't seem to know what to say. Avoiding his eyes, she bent down to the turtle, cooed gently at it. "Come on, big guy, you're going to be all right." She ran to the truck, opened the passenger side door then returned to heft the turtle together with Roman onto the vinyl bench seat.

Roman climbed in, and Leah took the driver's side. The engine coughed, then turned over. She had sand all over her clothes, and he realized for the first time, so did he. And neither of them had remembered to pick up their shoes.

On the way to Orchid Key, Leah kept up a steady stream of chatter as if trying to calm the turtle. And unbelievably, it seemed to be working. Well, for the turtle. Roman wasn't calm at all. He felt as if something was bubbling inside him the whole way, rising, filling his chest, and he was afraid to name it because he knew it was hope. He couldn't stop looking at Leah as she drove, captivated by her natural charm and energy. It was like seeing the old Leah again.

He felt as if he could stare at her forever, and he was sorry when they got to Orchid Key.

"I take it you've been here before," he said when she turned in at an unmarked gate in a stand of mangroves and the truck slid on the gravel to a stop in front of what looked like a run-down motel.

"I found a nest of baby turtles once," she told him. "Their mother had probably been hit by a boat or something. She'd washed up on the beach near the bar, and she was in bad shape. I knew about the turtle hospital, and I called them. They came out and took the babies. They tried to save the mother, but there wasn't anything they could do. Wait here.''

She jumped out of the truck, returning moments later with a guy in shorts and a Save-a-Turtle T-shirt.

Roman moved out of the way while the guy examined the turtle before asking Roman to help him get it inside. It was, he realized once they went in through the small lobby, a motel.

"It's run completely by volunteers," Leah explained when they'd delivered the turtle to one of the clinic rooms. "Come on, I'll show you."

She talked at warp speed as they walked, pointing out the holding pools for the turtles and the facilities where they received shots, IVs, even surgery. He couldn't keep his eyes off Leah.

"Some of the turtles live here full-time because they're too injured to go back into the water," she went on. "But whenever they can, they release them— but they tag them first. That's how we know this one's been here before." She stopped suddenly. They'd walked out back where a one-time motel guest pool had been turned into a saltwater turtle habitat. In the sun, her bright, dancing eyes seemed to shadow. "What? You keep—"

"What?"

"Looking at me!" She sounded annoyed.

"I just…haven't seen you this excited." Well, not in a long time, he added silently. "I bet you're one of the volunteers."

She shrugged. "I help out sometimes." He could see her closing up, as if she felt she'd revealed too much of herself to him. "We should get back to the bar,'' she said suddenly. ''I didn't plan on being gone this long.''

Before they left, one of the volunteers told them they'd probably have to amputate the wounded turtle's flipper. Leah was quiet on the way back to Thunder Key. When they got to the Shark and Fin, Roman went around the bar and got their shoes while Leah went inside.

''Oh,'' Joey said, polishing the counter and looking up at Leah as Roman walked in. ''I almost forgot. Someone called for you.''

''Who?'' She bent, slipped on her shoes.

''Don't know. He didn't leave his name.''

Roman didn't like the look that passed through Leah's eyes. He didn't like the fact that she'd been hung up on twice today, and that she had panic attacks. He didn't like that all the excitement that had been in her eyes at the turtle hospital was gone.

''Anyone else calls, let me take it,'' he told Joey. He couldn't stop thinking about Mark now. Would Mark call and ask for Leah? Just to see if it was really her? *I won't tell anyone about Leah—if that's really who it is.*

Leah cut him a frowning glance. Damn, she was as independent as ever.

''I'll get the phone, thank you,'' she said. ''You don't own the bar yet.''

''Something going on here I don't know about?'' Joey asked.

''She's had a couple hang-ups.''

''Wrong number, disconnection. It's no big deal,'' Leah inserted.

Joey looked at Roman.

"Hmm." The cook didn't look convinced. "Shanna called, too," he added. "She'll be in this evening. She's feeling better."

Roman guessed she must have been the missing waitress from lunch.

"Great." Leah headed toward the back. "I'm going to run upstairs for just a sec, then I'll help you prep for tonight," she said to Joey.

"We do an outdoor buffet on the beer deck," Joey explained to Roman. "Kind of a help-yourself thing. I grill shark, tuna,-whatever we have on hand. It's all you can eat, one set charge."

Leah was gone now. Joey's gaze narrowed on Roman. "If the phone rings," Joey said, "I'll get it."

Protective.

Roman understood how Joey felt. He was bugged about the calls, too. And more bugged that like Morrie, Joey seemed to have the inside track on Leah's trust.

Had he made any progress today in getting Leah to trust *him?* He headed for Morrie's office and put in a call to Mark's cell. His brother-in-law picked up.

"Did you call here?"

"What?"

"Did you call here? Did you ask for Leah?"

"You told me not to. Of course not." Mark sounded offended.

There was a crash upstairs. Roman's heart froze. He hung up the phone and bolted for the stairs.

Chapter 6

She barely even registered the crash of the lamp she'd knocked over when she backed into it.

Someone had been in her apartment.

It wasn't any one thing she noticed, but a combination of elements that shot a creeping, nameless dread up Leah's spine. The drawer she'd left slightly open was closed. The sheers were pulled straight. The tray of beads was on the floor, not on the coffee table. The pile of magazines on the kitchenette counter was stacked too neatly.

It was all just slightly off. Not how she'd left things. The bar was quiet, empty, and the back door had been unlocked. Between the walk on the beach and the trip to Orchid Key, they'd been gone for hours.

But why would someone come into her apartment? What could they want? Her thoughts reeled. Had she heard those words on the phone earlier today, or had they come from her nightmares, her unknowable past?

She'd backed up so quickly she'd pushed over the lamp on the table near the door. There was glass everywhere. The fixture had been an old-fashioned hurricane-style lamp. It belonged to Morrie, as did most of the furnishings in the small apartment. She felt shaky and scared and alone, and she wished desperately that Morrie were here now.

Then arms surrounded her. She jumped, let out a small scream.

"Leah, it's me."

Roman.

"Are you all right? The door was open, and I heard a crash—"

"I'm fine." No, she wasn't fine, not at all. Roman turned her in his arms, and she found herself nose to nose, so close to him she could have sworn she heard his heartbeat over her own. His eyes were steady, warm, concerned. And suddenly she felt like an idiot. "I knocked a lamp over." She swallowed thickly, her pulse still drumming. God, what must he think of her? She was a mess. This was the second time she'd broken something today. She turned back, looking at the room.

In the still quiet, with the bright daylight filtering through the pulled sheers, the room looked peaceful, normal, safe. Or was it Roman's arms that made her feel this way?

She twisted out of his arms. "I'm a klutz, that's all."

"Are you sure that's all?"

No, that wasn't all. There was more, so much more. But was it real?

Was she going crazy? None of it made sense. She

was accustomed to not remembering, to not knowing anything about her past, but now she was starting to feel something that scared her even more. Maybe she really was losing it. Had someone been in her apartment, or was she paranoid? Had someone said those nightmare-echo words to her on the phone this afternoon, or had she imagined it?

All this had begun since Roman Bradshaw had arrived in Thunder Key. Was he somehow connected to the phone calls, someone being in her apartment?

But Morrie had checked him out. Roman Bradshaw was for real, a zillion-dollar finance guy from Manhattan. But what did she really know about him besides that? Her initial gut feeling had been to not trust him. Had that gut feeling been right? But what connection could he possibly have to the phone calls? He'd been right there, in the bar, every time. He couldn't have made them.

The questions made her feel sick and angry.

"I'll just clean this up and be right down," she said quickly. Go away. She needed him to go away so she could pull herself together, think.

There was a broom and a dustpan in the tiny pantry closet in the kitchenette. She retrieved them, began brushing at the shattered glass with the broom.

"I'll do that," Roman suggested.

"No, I'm fine." She had the glass in a pile now. "You're not cleaning up another one of my messes." She knelt hurriedly, began pushing it into the dustpan. Brittle, brittle, just like glass—that's how she felt. She was so tense, she thought she might shatter into a million pieces if anyone so much as touched her.

Then Roman knelt, too, and put his hand over hers

on the dustpan. And she didn't shatter. His fingers felt
solid, warm. They were slightly bronzed from the sun
now. "Let me help," he said gently. "It's not a crime
to let someone do something for you, you know."

She swallowed thickly again and looked up at his
face. He was very close, and she was struck by the
vulnerability shining in his eyes now. And she had the
oddest sense that she would hurt his feelings if she
refused him. And she didn't want to hurt this man.
Her emotions were conflicted and she didn't know
what she was feeling. He was so near, she could see
every chiseled character line on his too-handsome-for-
her-nerves face. She'd be crazy to let herself be attracted to this man, any man, and yet…

The phone calls, the sense of someone having been
in her apartment—it was all but forgotten as she fell,
seemingly in some dreamy slow-mo, into his eyes.

He reached up with his other hand, stroked the side
of her cheek with his thumb. Gentle, caring, intent, the
way he'd been with the turtle. And fascinated somehow…by her. The way he'd looked at her during their
tour of the turtle hospital had almost given her a heart
attack. It had definitely had her stomach muscles dancing, her palms sweating, her head lightening. And now
she couldn't move, couldn't speak, couldn't do anything. His amazing gaze took her out of the moment,
into something that was familiar and strange all at
once.

She shut her eyes, overwhelmed. She could almost
feel him lean in, just so, and press his mouth to hers.
His lips would be warm, seeking, amazing. He would
make her feel secure and alive and *right*.

Some powerful connection seized her and she

couldn't have moved away to save her life. She wanted this touch, this feeling, to go on forever.

Heaven help her, she wanted him to kiss her. She already knew how it would feel, and she wanted it, wanted him. It made no sense, and the thought had her snapping her eyes open, jerking backward.

She stumbled, rocked off her balance, and dropped the dustpan, reaching back with her hands to keep from falling over.

A hot stab pierced her palm. She fell back on her bottom, lifted her hand. Blood dripped from the side of her hand. A shard of glass, missed in her too-hurried sweeping, protruded from the skin. She stared at it, immobilized for a beat from the mix of emotions and feelings and pain tangling inside her. Too much happening all at once. Her head felt light.

"Oh, God, Leah."

Roman grabbed her, somehow had her up on her feet without her really being aware it was happening. He drew her to the kitchenette. Flipping the light on over the sink, he examined her palm.

"I think I can get the glass out," he said. "It looks like just one piece. Then we can get the bleeding stopped. We're going to have to get you to a hospital. This needs stitches."

"There's a small local clinic downtown, near the library." She was having trouble thinking. "Dammit, I can't believe I did that to myself."

"This one's for people, not turtles, right?" Roman asked teasingly. "Okay, I'm going to pull this out. You might want to look away."

She squeezed her eyes shut, couldn't look. She knew he was just trying to distract her from what he was doing, but she responded anyway. "Yes, it's for people."

There was a quick tearing pain, then pressure. Opening her eyes, she found Roman pressing a paper towel over her hand. With his free hand, he tore off more disposable towels, began wrapping them around and around her hand.

"How are you doing?"

"Fantastic," she lied.

Leah's face was ashen, and Roman prayed she wasn't going to faint. She'd never been good with blood.

He put his arm around her and she didn't resist. He grabbed Morrie's keys without letting go of her arm. "Keep your arm elevated. That'll help stop the bleeding." Already the towel on her hand was spotting red. "Keep the pressure on it," he reminded her. He placed her other hand over the towel where the blood seeped through.

"I'm fine, you know," she said. "I probably could drive myself."

He ignored her. They went down the steps, into the bar. Joey came out of the kitchen.

"Everything okay? What happened?" Joey's eyes widened as he took in the makeshift bandage.

"Minor accident," Leah said. "I fell on some glass in my apartment." Her eyes swam with unshed tears. She was hurting more than she wanted to let on.

"I'm taking her to the clinic," Roman said. He got Leah out the door. He was half-afraid if Joey had two seconds to think, he'd insist on being the one to take Leah to the doctor.

The gas tank was practically sitting on empty after

their drive back and forth to Orchid Key. He opened the door on the passenger side for Leah. He moved around to the driver's side and climbed in. The vinyl bench seat was hot.

"I hope we have enough gas."

"It's not far," Leah said. "God, I feel stupid. I feel like I'm being such a pain. I can probably drive myself, you know," she repeated. "I'm not helpless."

"Not necessary. I'm here." He backed the truck up, pulled out of the parking lot. He drove down the road, over the humpbacked bridge, made a left onto the main drag and headed into town.

"It's right past the library," she said. "There." She pointed at a small building near a corner on the next block. He stopped at a stop sign, waiting as tourists crossed the street. Roman looked over at Leah. She was still pale. She'd closed her eyes and her lashes looked a little wet, but she wasn't crying. Nope, not Leah. She didn't like to cry.

She'd told him once that she'd taught herself not to cry in front of other people. For Leah, it had been out of character—she was so open, so free, wearing her heart on her sleeve. But there were things she'd never told him. Things about her past. Her childhood. She'd been an orphan, that's all he'd known. Whenever the conversation had strayed to her childhood, something dark and wounded would fill her eyes. She hadn't wanted to talk about it, and he hadn't pressed. Leah had lived in the here and the now.

And he'd let her, because exploring her emotions might have meant exploring his.

Now he wanted to know everything about her. Everything. And even if she had wanted to, now she couldn't tell him.

The irony killed him.

"It's okay to cry if it hurts," he said softly.

She opened her eyes. Her shiny depths reached right in and grabbed his heart with a tight fist.

"No, it's not." Her voice came out barely more than a whisper. "It's not okay. It's weak, and it makes people angry and—" She blinked, looked away. "I don't know what I'm saying."

She was so near, on the bench seat of the small cab of the pickup. He wanted to put his arms around her and hold her. He wanted to kiss her. And he wanted her to tell him why it was so hard for her to cry. What did she mean when she said it made people angry? He had no idea what she was talking about.

He'd had his chance to find out. He'd blown it. Guilt pressed down on him, dark and heavy. All he was to her now was a stranger.

A stranger who couldn't kiss her, no matter how desperate the longing inside him to do just that might be.

He drove across the street, turned into the small parking lot of the clinic.

"Let's go," he said. He got out of the truck, came around to open her door.

Inside, the clinic had a tiny waiting area that was blessedly empty.

Roman approached the woman behind the reception counter. "She cut her hand on a piece of glass, needs some stitches."

"I'll let the doctor know she's here." The receptionist took down Leah's name, then disappeared into the back. A nurse came out a few minutes later and called Leah inside.

"Do you want me to come in with you?" Roman asked.

"I'll be fine." She disappeared behind the closed door of the examining room.

Leah looked away while the nurse unwrapped the makeshift bandage. It took all her energy not to cry out while the wound was cleaned and examined. The nurse explained that she had to make certain no small bits of glass remained in the laceration.

It hurt like hell, that's all Leah knew.

The stitches were no better. The doctor sewed up the long cut in her hand while she squeezed her eyes shut and tried to pretend she was somewhere else... anywhere else. She searched her mind for some sense of safety where she could close herself off to the pain.

She was on a brick walkway in front of a small bungalow. A cigar maker's cottage, they called it, with traditional Bahamian-blue shutters and a tin roof. But all she cared about was the man beside her, holding her hand. The man who held her and made her whole in ways she'd never known possible.

Do you smell that? It's Spanish lime. Isn't it delicious? *she whispered, holding his hand in hers.*

You're delicious, *he said.*

He nipped at her lips, teased her mouth to kiss her so deeply he touched her very soul. Lime and musk and man swam together in her head. She felt his arousal pressed against her.

I want you, *she breathed against his mouth, and he swept her into his arms, carried her inside the bun-*

galow, stripped every stitch of clothing from her body, one slow piece at a time. And she knew that she loved him, intensely, unswervingly, forever. He was everything to her. He made everything that was wrong in her life into something right.

Naked, she wasn't satisfied. He had to be naked, too. She peeled off his jeans and tore back his shirt. Looking wasn't enough, though—she had to touch. She pressed her face against the strong muscles of his chest, his heartbeat penetrating the daze of seduction as her hands roamed down his body, pulling him atop her, tumbling them both onto the big bed.

Then he was touching her, his warm fingers seeking her feminine heat, intimate and tender. She trembled as he entered her, hard and fast and deep—

"All done."

Leah opened her eyes, shocked. The doctor patted her uninjured arm.

"You're going to be just fine," he said. "That should heal up nicely." He gave her directions for tending the wound, changing her bandages. "I'll give you prescriptions for pain relief and antibiotics. I'll need to see you back in a week to remove the stitches."

He set about scribbling on a pad.

Cold pain washed over Leah, but it didn't come from her hand. The harsh light of the examining room stunned her eyes, and something fisted tightly around her chest. Oh, God, where had her mind gone? Where had that dream come from? It had been so real.

"Here you go." The doctor handed her the prescriptions.

Leah walked from the examining room. Roman

stood up. He looked dangerously sexy, and worried. A lazy fan turned the air in the waiting area, but it didn't do that great a job on a hot Keys day. At the reception counter, she realized with a start that she hadn't brought her wallet.

"I didn't bring any money."

"I've got it." Roman pulled out his billfold. "Are you all right?"

"Yes. Just had a few stitches." She felt shy and strange as she briefly met his eyes. The weirdness of the thoughts she'd experienced while being stitched up still enveloped her. It had been a daydream, a fantasy, a way to escape the pain, but it had been so vivid. So real. Except the man in her dream hadn't had a face.

Roman paid the bill, and they went out to the truck. The fresh air knocked the cobweb-like clouds from her mind, leaving her with the sharp sting of the wound.

"I'll pay you back," she said, trying to focus away from the pain again.

"It's partly my fault. So forget it. I think I startled you, made you lose your balance."

"It wasn't your fault," she argued. "And it's no big deal. I've been hurt a lot worse and lived to tell about it." She bit her lip, not sure where that had come from, but knowing it was true. She'd had broken bones, burns, cuts. She turned her arm over, looked at a small trail of very faint scars that marred the underside. Cigarette burns, she knew abruptly, and the thought shocked her.

Roman opened the truck door for her then went around to slide in behind the wheel. She reached up, fingers trembling now, and ran her fingers along her hairline, felt another thin scar there. She'd noticed it before, of course, but suddenly it ached to the touch. She dropped her hand, her finger seeming almost burned by the scar.

Roman didn't start the engine. He sat there, his gaze on her grim in the small confines of the truck's cab. Then he moved, touched the scar in her hairline.

"What happened to you?" he asked. "How did you get this scar?"

A dizzy wash of something cold came down over her. She heard herself answering, but it was as if she was hearing someone else speak. Not her. "I was fifteen. My foster father hit me because I had disobeyed him. I'd hidden eye shadow and lipstick in my school backpack, and he picked me up early and found me wearing it. I looked like a whore, that's what he said. When we got home, he followed me inside and hit me from behind so hard I fell into the refrigerator handle. It cut my head open."

The words had burst out of her, and she had no idea where they'd come from. How had she suddenly known that story? Somehow, telling Roman was dangerous and safe all at once. She shouldn't tell him anything. She'd determinedly kept her secrets to herself for eighteen months on Thunder Key, confiding only in Viv and Morrie.

But she found herself wanting to tell Roman Bradshaw things she hadn't even told them. Things she didn't even understand or remember till she spoke the words. Why? What was it about this stranger that made her open up when she knew better?

Her past was a dark, frightening danger. A black hole that could spiral her deep into a place she didn't want to go. There were things about herself she didn't want to remember. That was her gut instinct, and that was enough.

But she was starting to remember things. And she was terrified.

"Oh, God, Leah." Roman's eyes glistened in the shadows of the truck cab. He looked grim and unforgiving, and like he could kill someone. "I had no idea."

Her heart pounded painfully inside her chest, and she shook all over now. She felt dirty for some reason. *It's all your fault.* She heard her foster father's words in her head, over and over. It was another memory—disjointed and out of place—or was it? Was it real, or imagined? What about the dreamy lovemaking with the faceless man? And the voice on the phone? It all tangled through her, hopelessly lost in the maze of her mind. She wanted to block the memory of that awful nightmare voice, but it just kept coming back, relentless.

I know who you are. I know what you've done. Who did that voice belong to? It wasn't her foster father. It was someone else.

Don't think you can get away with this. Don't think you can ruin my life— The memories came to her like disjointed audiotapes. What did it all mean? Piercing pain slammed into her temples.

"I want to beat the crap out of your foster father," Roman said, bitterness filling his low voice. In that moment he looked fully capable of violence.

"You can't. He's dead." Oh, God. Why did that terrify her so much? She was shaking more than ever. Some dark fury burst to the surface. She fought it back with all her might.

Blood, screams…

The tears she wasn't allowed to cry spilled down her cheeks. She grabbed at the door handle. All she wanted to do was run, as far away from the past as she could go.

Chapter 7

Roman caught her before she could get the door open.

He could see she was desperate to not let him see her cry. She was going to get out on the damn street to prevent him from seeing her do anything that weak.

He held on to her and never wanted to let her go. What the hell was he doing? Every time he touched her, it only got worse.

How long could he hide his feelings from her? Especially when she was opening up to him this way suddenly. He hadn't been prepared for what she'd told him about her past. She'd remembered something. How long before she remembered *him?* How much time did he have with her before he had to risk losing her forever by telling her the truth?

"I need to be alone," she said, pushing away from him. She rubbed her good hand down her face, first one cheek then the other, removing the traces of tears. She sounded so stiff, so formal. All pulled together. Damn her. "That's all. Just take me back to the bar. You've done more than enough. I really appreciate it and—"

"I don't think being alone is what you need." He wanted to kiss her, make all her heartache go away. And that was impossible. But he sure as hell wasn't leaving her alone.

"You don't know what I need."

She was right. He didn't know what she needed. If he'd known what she needed, he would have asked her to open up to him during their marriage. He wouldn't have let his own wife suffer in silence, never so much as asking a single question about her childhood beyond where she grew up or if her parents were alive. She hadn't wanted to talk about it, and he hadn't pressed. Leah'd had a charming way of living in the present, and she'd made it so easy for him to let her.

Don't ask, don't tell. That was the Bradshaw way when it came to emotions.

"I know a little about keeping your feelings to yourself," he said. "You can't make feelings go away just by hiding them."

"Oh, yes, you can."

He thought for a minute she was going to say more, but she just stared out the passenger window, her expression stoic. He wanted her to tell him that she'd lost her memory, that she had these flashes that were clearly coming back to her.

Most of all, he wanted her to trust him.

"Not completely," he said. "You can't make them go away completely."

She shrugged. "Good enough for government work. That's one of Morrie's favorite sayings." Her eyes, red and still damp, met his. Her brief breakdown might have never happened—her emotions were all tucked away in some secret place he'd never been.

"You said he was like a father."

"Morrie's the only father I've ever known."

Her birth parents had died when she was very young. Leah had grown up in a series of foster homes. That was all Roman knew.

"How'd you meet Morrie?" He still hadn't started the engine. The windows were down, and people passed by on the sidewalks. But they were in their own world, inside the truck's cab.

"On the beach." She gazed out the windows, watching the tourists in their colorful Florida garb. The sound of stirring palms in the breeze mixed with the noise of cars and voices. But it all felt very distant. "I had just—arrived—in the Keys, and he offered me a job, a place to live. He was kind, generous. I was pretty much on my own, and he gave me the new start I needed."

"How did you get here?" He was curious about everything that had happened to her in the last eighteen months, especially going back to the night Leah had disappeared.

Her answer didn't satisfy him.

"Bus," was all she said.

"Why did you come here?"

She looked back at him now. "Some things just feel…right. You know what I mean? You don't have to know why."

Roman's heart wrenched. *Why* was all he wanted to know. He held her gaze for a long moment.

There was still one trace of moisture on her cheek, and he lifted his hand, slowly, very slowly, and wiped it away.

"Are you happy here, Leah?" He wondered if all the longing, desire, need in his heart showed in his eyes. All he knew was he couldn't look away. She smelled deliciously sweet. Her skin was so soft beneath his touch. She felt impossibly wonderful.

"Yes," she said finally. "I'm happier than I've ever been."

He was dying. He had to be dying. His heart couldn't hurt this much without killing him. Yep, he should have stopped while he was ahead, when she'd told him Thunder Key felt *right*.

She remembered the foster father who'd brutalized her, but not Roman. *I'm happier than I've ever been.*

He dropped his hand, leaned back into his own place on the truck's bench seat. It took all his power to keep his emotions out of his voice.

"I need to get you home," he said. "I'll pick up the prescriptions after I drop you off. Just tell me where the pharmacy is."

He started the engine and drove back to the bar.

Leah's hand was killing her, but she wanted to work. No way was she going to sit up in her apartment, leave Joey and the waitresses shorthanded and wait for another freaky phone call. She could still manage the taps, just a bit slower than usual. She had to explain what had happened to her hand about two million times before the night was over. Everyone asked.

She answered their questions vaguely, and tried not to think about everything that was bothering her. A man sat at the end of the bar fiddling with a digital camera, and at one point, she could have sworn he took a picture of her. It wasn't uncommon for tourists who stumbled onto the colorful, Keysy bar to take photos of it, but somehow she didn't think he was a tourist. And she didn't think he'd taken a picture of the bar. He'd taken a picture of *her*.

Her imagination had been working overtime lately, though, and she worked to shake off the weird feeling he gave her.

He wore a windbreaker. He took a cell phone out of it and spoke into it several times while watching her. Once, she thought she glimpsed something dark tucked into the waistband of his jeans, beneath the light jacket. It looked like a gun, and her blood froze. She mentioned it to Joey, and he asked the man if he was carrying a concealed weapon.

The man left without answering Joey's question. The uneasiness of his presence remained behind, filtering through Leah's evening.

Maybe she'd been wrong. Maybe that wasn't a gun she'd seen. Maybe he'd just been taking a touristy photo of the bar. Maybe she'd just offended a customer.

But she was glad when he was gone.

Roman had gone back out for her prescriptions, but she knew the pain medication might make her sleepy, so she'd decided to wait until closing time to take it.

Roman insisted on staying to work the buffet, which kept him mostly out on the beer deck, to Leah's relief.

The day had been exhausting, strange, and she still didn't know what to think about any of it. The phone calls, the strange man in the bar…and Roman Bradshaw. He was so gentle and haunted, and yet somehow terribly forbidding all at once. With every moment that passed, she knew she could very easily let herself fall for a man who could only ever be her friend.

And that was bad. Very bad.

But even so, the very sight of him made her heart beat faster. Worse, he somehow touched an emotional chord within her, had memories spilling to the surface.

"I'm going up," she said in general when the bar was empty. Shanna and Joey had things just about cleaned up. The other waitresses had already left.

"I'll lock up," Joey said.

"How's your hand?" Roman asked.

"Fine." She picked up the pharmacy bag from the shelf below the bar. "Thanks again," she told him.

She locked the back door near the office and stairs to the apartment. Leaning against it, she let out a sigh. No more leaving the back door unlocked, period. She'd gotten lax, living in the friendly Keysy environment. Whether someone had been in her apartment or not, whether the strange man in the bar—who might or might not have been carrying a concealed weapon—was watching her or not, it wasn't a good idea to leave a nonpublic door of the bar unlocked, ever, even when there were people inside. The door that led to her apartment was isolated, set off from the dining patio, hidden by large shrubbery.

Upstairs, she peeled off her clothes, stepped into the

pajamas she wore at night. The apartment was quiet, and she felt exhausted and restless all at once.

She knew what was wrong. She was afraid to go to sleep, afraid of what more she might remember or dream. Too often, she had nightmares.

Sitting in the middle of the pulled-out Murphy bed, she let her fingers trace again the faint marks on her arm. She knew they were cigarette burns. From that foster father or another one? How many foster homes had she lived in—and why? Was that what her mind was blocking? A terrible childhood?

Or something else?

I know who you are. I know what you've done.

What had she done? *Who* was she?

Don't think you can ruin my life.

Whose life had she been in the position of ruining?

She knew, somewhere deep and hidden, that it had to be more than that she'd had a foster parent who abused her. *She* had done something.

Could remembering it be any worse than what she was dealing with now? She turned off the light, shut her eyes. She hadn't taken the pain pill. She'd started to take it, but somehow couldn't bring herself to put it in her mouth. It was one of those instinctive things, like cats and peas. She didn't like pain pills.

Sleep didn't come easily. Instead, she kept thinking—what if remembering *was* worse?

She drifted, half-awake for a long time, thinking back over the day. Walking on the pier with Roman. Lunch with Roman. The beach, and hiking up into the lighthouse. The trip to the turtle hospital.

Sleep finally folded her in, dark and heavy.

She was in the lighthouse, trapped. Hurricane winds

*and tides rushed against the walls. Creaking of mortar
and stone, and then water—pouring in. Choking. She
was choking.*

*Then she was in a car, underwater. She flailed
against the wheel, pounded at the closed window. Pan-
icking, her hand gripped the door handle, pushing,
pushing.*

*The door wouldn't move. She was stuck. Drowning.
Then the door burst open—only it wasn't a car door,
it was the door to a house now.*

*A man lay on the floor, dead, blood pooling around
his flaccid body. She felt something cold, heavy in her
hand, and she looked down and saw a gun.*

Leah sat bolt upright. It took harrowing beats for
her to realize the darkness surrounding her was only
her own night-draped apartment.

She sank back against the cold sheet. She couldn't
stop shaking.

Roman woke early. The orange-rimmed horizon filtered in through the patio sheers. He made coffee in
the small automatic coffeemaker in the bungalow,
downed one cup and laced up his running shoes.

She was on the bar's back stoop when he showed
up. She was locking up with a key hooked to an elastic
wristband. He was glad to see her being careful.

God help him, he was just glad to see her. Every
day, he opened his eyes and was grateful that Leah
was alive and on Thunder Key. Even if she didn't want
him in the end, he could learn to live with it. Just
knowing that she was alive was enough—almost.

Constant in the back of his mind was the chance

that she wouldn't want him once she knew the truth of who he was.

Not that he was ready to give up yet. Not by a long shot. And he was planning to make damn sure nothing else happened to her.

He was worried about those phone calls. He needed more time. It was too soon to tell her ·the truth. But the more he thought about those phone calls, the more he thought about the bizarre circumstances of her disappearance eighteen months ago…

What if it was all connected? Once the thought had occurred to him, he couldn't shake it.

"Morning."

She looked startled. "Oh, Roman. Hi." She took in his running gear. "I was just about to go for a run."

"Mind if I tag along?"

She looked as if she *did* mind. But she also looked exhausted. Her eyes were rimmed with shadows, her face too pale.

"How's the hand?" he asked as they took off. He knew she had a regular routine down the beach, into town. She'd stop off for a café con leche at the Cuban coffeehouse, then walk back to the Shark and Fin.

"Great. Much better."

"No more weird phone calls? No more accidents?"

"Nope. I'm sorry about everything yesterday. I'm sure I gave you the wrong impression, breaking everything in sight, having a panic attack, crying." She looked embarrassed and angry with herself. "You just decided to look into buying the bar on my worst day ever. But—it's a new day." She increased her pace. "Don't feel like you have to keep up with me."

Damn her, she was trying to lose him. And she was

completely closed up. Whatever she was thinking, feeling, no way was she letting him in.

And she looked exhausted.

"I'm in shape." He increased his pace to match hers.

She gave him a quick sideways glance. Her cheeks were still pale, but her eyes were hot. Then she looked straight ahead again. Kept running.

"You know, that whole phone thing was probably just messed-up lines," she said. "Happens sometimes out here in the Keys."

"Maybe," he said. Who was she trying to convince—him or herself?

"I don't need any self-appointed bodyguards."

"Wouldn't dream of it," he said, keeping pace with her, measuring his long strides against her smaller ones.

She stopped so abruptly Roman skidded in the sand turning back. Arms on her hips, she glared at him. He closed the distance between them with a quick stride.

"Then why are you here?" she demanded. "I run alone. That's how I like it."

"I don't think it's safe."

"Okay, the truth comes out."

"You had some strange phone calls. You don't know it was phone problems."

She looked away, shielding her eyes. She gazed out at the water, avoiding him.

"This isn't New York City," she said tensely. "It's sleepy little Thunder Key."

"Can you think of any reason that someone would be harassing you?" He waited, but she didn't answer.

"If there's something going on, something frightening you—*anything*—you have to tell me."

A bird swooped over the water, plucked a fish from the blue depths. The breeze fingered Leah's hair.

"I don't *have* to do anything," she said stubbornly.

"I'm not going to let anything happen to you, Leah. No matter what I have to do. I'm not going to let you be hurt."

Her eyes darkened with something akin to confusion as she swung on him now.

"Why?" she demanded suddenly. "Why do you care so much?"

"I can't stand to think that you might be in danger. I don't want anything else to happen to you. Not now, not ever."

"Anything *else?*"

He was scaring her, he knew it. And he felt so lost, as lost as she looked in that moment.

"Do I know you?" she demanded, not for the first time. "I look at you…" Her voice trailed away, almost broke. He barely heard the rest of her words. "I *feel* as if I know you. And it just makes me want to—"

"What?" He grabbed her arms. "What does it make you feel?"

"Let me go!" She tried to twist out of his arms.

And that was when he noticed the man in the trees. He was standing just inside the hammock of mangroves lining the beach. The sun caught the lens of a camera pointed directly at them.

Then Roman saw the gun tucked into the waistband of his jeans.

Leah noticed his cold stare over her shoulders,

stopped struggling, turned her head. She saw the man, too.

The man in the trees sank back, disappeared. Roman wanted to chase after him, question him, but he knew he'd never catch him. The man had been maybe twenty yards or more from them, and the woods were thick.

He didn't want to let go of Leah.

"That's the man from the bar," Leah said. She looked back at Roman. "He was taking photos yesterday. He was taking photos of— God, I thought he was taking photos of *me*."

"Why?" Roman asked, cold dread snaking through his gut. He held on to her tight. "Why, Leah?"

"I don't know." She shivered in the warm morning breeze. She looked exhausted enough to collapse any minute. "He was at the bar last night. I felt as if he was watching me. I thought he had a gun in his jacket. Joey went to speak to him, and he left. And I thought someone was in my apartment yesterday when we were on the beach. I thought my apartment had been searched."

"You didn't tell me. You didn't tell me about any of this. Only the phone calls."

"I wasn't sure," she whispered in an aching voice. "I thought I might be paranoid, or imagining it."

It killed him to see her confused and scared, and no matter what happened next, he couldn't let her be in danger. Not when he could help her.

Even if it ruined any chance he'd ever have of winning her love.

But he couldn't think about that now. Leah's life could be in danger. Someone was stalking her—calling her, watching her, photographing her. Someone who had a gun.

And it could all be connected to the past. The past she didn't remember. Her strange disappearance.

There was no more time for taking things slow. There was no more time for anything…but the truth. The wonderful, awful truth.

He looked into her soulful eyes and prayed that she wouldn't hate him when this day was over.

"I want you to come back to the hotel with me. And then there's something I have to tell you."

His words were ominous, as was the look on his face. Leah had to know what he had to say.

The sensation of surrealness overtook her, and all she wanted to do was run, despite how tired she was. He took her back the way they'd come, then up the deserted road from the bar. They flew over the little bridge, then turned down the mangrove path through the trees to the other side of the island.

They came out of the trees, into the balmy brightness. She'd seen the White Seas from a distance, but she'd never been up close to it. The hotel itself was classic Bahamian style, but Roman led her around the back, away from the multistoried hotel, toward the individual guest bungalows.

The guest bungalows were restored little cigar maker's cottages. Traditional tin roofs, blue shutters and porches. They slowed to a walk, and Roman took her hand as he led her down the bricked paths lined with sculptures. Latan palms and Barbados cherry trees and Spanish limes scented the air.

Dizzy shock spun through her.

Do you smell that? It's Spanish lime. Isn't it delicious?

You're delicious.

He nipped at her lips, teasing her mouth open—

Oh, God. She stopped so abruptly, Roman, his hand still tightly holding hers, pulled her forward before he realized she wasn't following and she almost fell.

"Leah." His dark eyes pierced her soul.

"I've been here before," she whispered thickly. Fear, icy and heavy, washed down her veins.

"Yes," he said.

"Do I know you?" she asked him again. Her pulse jumped erratically. It felt like forever and a split instant for him to answer. "Do you know me?"

"Yes," he said again. "Yes."

She ripped her hand from his. She wasn't thinking, only feeling, reacting. She ran from him, past the bungalows, off the path, onto the beach.

The panic attack doubled her over, heaving her to the sand. Sick. She was going to be sick. She stumbled to her feet, kept running.

"No, Leah, stop!"

He was chasing her. And no way in hell was she going to be able to outrun him, not when she was about to throw up any second.

But she couldn't stop trying.

"Leah," he called again, and this time he caught her.

They stumbled to the sand together. He did his best to protect her, twisting so that she ended up falling on top of him. His arms held her tightly, safely.

No, not safe. He wasn't safe. He was a liar. She'd

asked him before if she knew him, and he'd said no. And now—

"Let me go."

"No, Leah." He held on even as she struggled. "I can't let you go."

"Why? *Who are you?*"

He twisted again, pinning her on the sand. He wasn't hurting her, but he wasn't letting her go. She felt sand against her back and the pounding of his heart against hers.

He stared into her eyes, and his looked as wild as she knew hers must in this moment. Cold fear and a strange hope tangled inside her chest, wrapping her in something so unreal it was like another dream. Another nightmare.

"I'm your husband."

Chapter 8

"That's insane." Her eyes were huge, shocky.

"No." Roman was afraid to let go of her, terrified she'd disappear, evaporate before his very eyes. Like in his dreams. "You're Leah. Leah Bradshaw. *My wife.*"

"Your wife is dead."

He held her tortured gaze for a long beat. Steady. He had to be steady. He had to convince her that he was real, that she was real, that he was telling the truth. He couldn't come on like a crazy man. But he was the furthest thing from calm. He was scared to death.

"I *thought* my wife was dead. But you're alive, Leah. You're alive. And I've found you."

"No," she whispered hoarsely. She contorted her body, struggling to free herself from his hold. "No!"

"Leah, stop. Listen to me." He gripped her. She turned her head away. "I'm telling you the truth."

"No!"

"Yes! Look at me, Leah! We were married. We're still married. You're not Leah Wells and you know it. Leah Wells doesn't exist. I don't know what happened that night. I don't know why you can't remember. But you know I'm telling you the truth. You remember being trapped underwater. Don't you?"

She turned her head toward him. Her gaze was lost and scared, but something flickered in her eyes, something tiny and barely noticeable, but it was there. She was listening.

"I lost my wife in a car accident." He kept going, trying his damnedest to slow down for her sake. "Her car went over a bridge, into the water. They never found her. They never found *you*. They told me you were dead, drowned, washed away in the storm. But I found you here, Leah. On Thunder Key. We spent our honeymoon here at the White Seas. You know you've been here before."

He could feel the shaking of her body. Her eyes— bright, shiny, confused—tore at him. What could he say? What could he do? He knew what he wanted to do—crush his mouth against hers, kiss her until she remembered him, until she couldn't *not* remember him. Make her body know what her mind had blocked out.

Close. She was so close. Her lips were a breath away. He could feel her heart pounding.

"You know you've been here before," he said. "Somewhere deep inside, you know you've been here. And you know that you know me. You said you felt it, every time you looked at me. We were lovers, Leah. Husband and wife. We had a life together. I gave you that bracelet you're wearing on our honeymoon—right here at the White Seas. I'm not crazy. You have to believe me.''

She wasn't struggling now, just staring at him, and sudden awareness crackled between them. He knew all the desire he felt for her had to be burning in his eyes. And in her eyes—a flare of something. Desperation, and it matched his own. She was his wife, and somewhere inside, she knew it. No way was he giving up.

''I don't know what to believe,'' she whispered, raw.

''Yes, you do,'' he said. ''You know this is true. You know you feel this connection between us.''

He watched his words register in her eyes, and he couldn't stop himself from reaching for what he'd wanted for so long. He claimed her mouth, sweeping his tongue inside at the immediate, shocked parting of her lips. He tasted her teeth, her tongue, her amazing sweet familiarity. He felt alive, alive like he hadn't felt in eighteen horrible months. And happy. For one incredible heartbeat, he was happy. God, she was kissing him back, and nothing in his life had ever been sweeter or more agonizing.

A weight of emotion filled his chest. Desire hit him with a rush, low in his gut. But with what little lucidity he had left, he sensed her stiffen, change, felt the frantic push of her hand against his chest.

''No, oh, my God,'' she breathed against his mouth, and tore away, scrambling to her feet.

''Leah, wait.'' He went after her. She pivoted toward him, hugging her arms to her body, a fragile form silhouetted against the sea. Staring at him as if she was scared to death of him.

She could have no idea how she was killing him. He wanted to spill his guts right here, right now, but that would only frighten her more. He wanted to hold her, kiss her again, bury himself inside her. He wanted a lot of things he couldn't have.

"Come inside with me," he said, his voice husky with emotion. "We need to talk, Leah."

The sun felt cold on his face in spite of the growing warmth of the day. She looked so scared.

"I can't. I need time."

"You're out of time. *We're* out of time. I don't know what happened the night your car went over the bridge, Leah, but if I've found you, there's a chance someone else has found you, too. Those phone calls, the man watching you, taking pictures—it could be connected to the past, to the night you disappeared."

"It was an accident. The car going over the bridge was an accident. You said so yourself." But even as she spoke the words, he could hear the doubt in her own voice, the fear.

"I can take you to see doctors who can help you. Come to New York with me—"

Her eyes sparked. "No."

"Fine. Then we won't go to New York. There are doctors in Miami."

"No."

Her thick, chin-length hair tangled across her cheeks. Vaguely he was aware of other people on the beach now. People from the hotel. Watching them. They were creating a scene, beginning to attract attention.

"Why not?"

"I don't know who to trust, what to believe."

"Trust me. Believe me."

"You lied to me!"

Roman reached in his back pocket, pulled out his wallet. He opened it, flipped past his driver's license, to the one photo it contained.

He gave it to Leah.

Leah forgot to breathe. She could barely think. Her mind rioted with so many different emotions, she was lost in the tangled mess of them.

The small, wallet-size photograph took her breath away. The image was of a man in a suit, Roman, and a woman, her eyes shining up at him, in a wedding dress. The woman was a stranger to her eyes—and yet she knew without a doubt that the woman was her.

She had been his wife. She had stood beside him in a wedding gown, spoken vows.

She was Leah Bradshaw.

He was telling the truth about that at least. All this time he had been grieving for her—and she was alive, here on Thunder Key. It blew her mind.

So many things he'd said over the past few days about his wife raced through her mind. She was that wife he'd spoken about. It felt impossible to her. And yet, there she was, in this photograph. And something, somewhere inside her had known she knew him.

That scared her the most. She didn't have to believe him to know he was telling the truth. Something inside her *knew* it was true. And when he'd kissed her…

She had known then, too. *Oh, God, she was his wife.* But wrapping her head around that fact left her reeling.

"You could be in danger, Leah. I want you away from here. If you don't want to go to New York, we'll go somewhere else. Until we're sure you're safe."

"I have a life here." *No.* It was all she could think—*no.* This was her home, and the past eighteen months were all she could remember. "I have a job. I'm not leaving Thunder Key with you." How could she go anywhere with this stranger? She was still reeling at the knowledge that she had been his *wife.* Her whole world was tumbling into chaos. Thunder Key was all she had to hold on to.

"Then you stay here with me, at the White Seas," he said.

"No," Leah said immediately, almost violently. "The bar is my home. I'm not leaving my home." She paused a moment. "It's all I know."

Rage and grief welled up in Roman. This was his wife, and she was afraid to be with him. It hurt like hell, but he had to face it. It was how she felt. The bar had been her sanctuary for eighteen months. But it might not be safe now. And she had to face that.

"Your home isn't safe," he said grimly. "Look, if—" He couldn't believe what he had to say next. "If you're afraid I'm going to kiss you, or anything else, you don't have to be. I lost my head, I admit it. I kissed you. You're my *wife.* We've kissed, hell, a thousand times. We've made love. Leah, I just want to keep you safe. You don't have to be afraid of me. I give you my word, what just happened—" That kiss. "It won't happen again."

She said nothing. She didn't believe him, didn't trust him, still.

"Leah, I swear to you that the only thing I've lied

about is who we were to each other. We need to find
out what's going on, who's watching you and why.
The apartment isn't safe now.''

"Then I'll go to Marian's," she suggested. "Or
Shanna's or Viv's.''

He didn't know who Viv was, but he didn't stop to
ask. "And put them in danger?''

Her eyes widened. He realized she hadn't gotten
that far in her thinking.

"Then you can stay at the bar," she said. "There's
a cot in Morrie's office—''

"I need to be with you, Leah, not in another room,
on another floor. I don't want you alone, at all, until
we know what's going on. At the bar there are people
coming and going, late at night. It's isolated. The hotel
is safer.''

"You don't know that." But there was doubt in her
eyes, and a flash of fear. Of him? Or of herself? She'd
responded when he'd kissed her, whether she would
admit that or not. A violent, almost unstoppable ex-
plosion of need—on both their parts.

Was that the real reason she didn't want to stay with
him? Was she afraid of how much he wanted her—or
of how much she wanted him?

"You know as well as I do that the apartment isn't
safe," he said. "Someone's already broken in, and
they might not be finished. At the hotel, there's security around the clock. It's the best choice, Leah, and
you know it.''

He watched the struggle in her eyes. She looked
exhausted and fragile, and he wanted nothing more
than to wrap her in his arms and keep her safe forever.

Slowly she took a breath, squared her slender shoulders. "All right," she said. "I'll stay with you. For now."

The bungalow was decorated in what the hotel called "upscale Cuban" style, colorful, tasteful and intimately designed. They walked past the king-size bed, the huge mound of pillows partially hidden by flowing mosquito netting reminding him that once they'd shared that secret place together. Made love. Right here in this very room.

Don't go there, Roman. He shut the memories down.

"You said you spent your honeymoon at the White Seas." Her voice sounded strained, odd. He could actually feel her anger, pain, radiating in the close quarters.

His gut clenched. "We stayed here for a week," he said. "You remembered something...when we stood in the pathway outside."

"I remembered the Spanish lime. The scent of it." She looked out at the beach view from the garden doors, then back at him.

"I'll tell you anything you want to know," he said. "Surely there are things you want to know—about yourself, about us."

A long beat passed. Maybe she wasn't ready. Maybe he was a fool to think she'd ever be ready. He was a fool to hope. And yet he couldn't stop hoping.

Maybe the pieces of information he could provide would jog something in her mind.

"How long were we married?" she asked finally.

"Six months."

"We lived in New York?"

"Yes. Manhattan. We have—had—an apartment across from Central Park. You designed clothing for a specialty boutique. You were part of an artist co-op."

She walked ahead of him, toward the sitting area. "I knew I was an artist, that I designed clothes. I wanted to design jewelry, too." She stopped in front of the garden doors, looked back at him. "I remember the odd detail without knowing why. I know that I'm a horrible cook. I know I love cats but I'm allergic."

She remembered those tidbits, odd details as she called them, but she didn't remember him.

He shoved down the pain. "I was amazed to find you running a bar and grill. You were always trying to cook, but you burned everything. You would get distracted, run off and do something else and forget supper. You were always impulsive like that. Then you'd try to sneak in takeout."

"You said you had a lot of regrets about your marriage."

Your marriage. Like it was all his, not hers.

"Yes." His heart slammed, painfully. "Everything I told you about our marriage was the truth."

She pulled out a chair, sat at the table. She placed the photograph he'd given her on the table, folded her hands in her lap and stared straight at him, looked scared, brittle.

"Tell me," she said, "about me."

He sat across from her. "You're Leah Bradshaw. You were Leah Conner when we met. You're twenty-seven years old. Your birthday is April thirteenth. We were married on August thirteenth. You loved the number thirteen—said it was your lucky number."

There was a sharp flare in her eyes for a moment, then her gaze shuttered again.

"Leah Conner." She repeated the name as if it felt uncomfortable on her tongue. "Where did we meet?"

"In the park. You were running. I was a runner, too. You would sit down afterward on a bench and watch the horse-drawn carriages. You loved the flowers in their manes. You loved to just…watch them. It was a small, everyday thing that I was so used to, I never noticed. But you watched the horses every day as if for the first time. You noticed all the little things, all the time. One day I sat down beside you and we started talking. And that was it. We were married six weeks later." He had been completely, off-his-rocker taken with her from the moment they'd met.

"Did we have a big wedding?" She gazed down at the photo now as if trying to see into the mind of the woman pictured there, the woman she'd once been.

"No. It was small. In the park. Just my family, and a few of your friends from the artist co-op. One of the other artists, Nikki Bates, was your maid of honor. She was your roommate before we got married. You shared a little flat with her in Chelsea." He watched for any flicker of recognition at her friend's name, but saw none.

"What about my family?"

"You said you had no family. You told me your parents had died when you were a child. You were raised in a series of foster homes."

She was silent.

He wanted to touch her so badly, but he knew she didn't want the physical contact with him and truthfully, he couldn't bear it, either. It only made him want more of what he couldn't have.

"Where was I from?" she asked. "Before New York?"

"You told me you came from a small town in Virginia near the beach."

"Do you have more pictures?"

"In New York."

She was quiet again, staring down at the one photo she held.

"Let's just get this over with," she said suddenly. "Let's find out what's going on."

Let's just get this over with.

Fine. They'd get this the hell over with. "Then we have to start with the night your car went over the bridge," he said as if she hadn't just twisted the knife already killing him. "This is going to mean seeing a doctor whether you want to or not, Leah. If you want to get this over with, that is." Her face tensed, but she didn't protest. "And we're going to have to contact the police. Your apartment was broken into."

She looked pale, fragile, but he knew she was strong, always had been. "I don't remember much... from that night," she began. "I remember the water. I didn't know—" Her brow furrowed, and despair flickered across her face. "You said your wife—"

"You."

She seemed to swallow thickly. "I... It was a car accident," she corrected. "The car went into a river."

Still, she spoke as if the accident had happened to someone else, not her.

"Your car went over a bridge," he clarified.

"How? Were there other cars involved? Some sort of pileup?"

He realized, despite her reluctance, that she was desperate for information. She'd spent eighteen months trapped in a mystery. He wished he had more answers for her.

"There were no other cars involved, as far as anyone knew. There were no witnesses to the accident. It was late, stormy, and the visibility was low on the roads that night. The next day someone reported seeing the broken railing, and they found your car in the river. You were just gone, completely gone. They finally convinced me you'd been swept away in the storm. They convinced me you were dead."

She said nothing, and he yearned again to reach out to her. But that would be a mistake.

"Where was I going?" she asked.

You were leaving me. With divorce papers.

"I was working late," he said instead. This was true, of course. "I don't know where you were going. Tell me what the first thing is you're sure of that you remember."

"Running. I was running along the highway. I was soaked, but it was raining. I don't think I realized then that I'd been in the river. I didn't know how I got wet. Maybe it had just been the rain. But later—"

"What happened later?"

"Nightmares."

He wanted to know more about her nightmares, but she shuddered when she spoke. Her hands were on the tabletop now, and she twisted her fingers together. He could see her knuckles whitening on her unbandaged hand.

"You told me you came to Thunder Key on a bus," he probed.

"Not all the way. I hitched a ride with a trucker."

She'd hitched. The risk in that hit him full in the chest. She'd dragged herself, somehow, out of the wreckage of her drowning car, memory destroyed, and climbed into a rig with a stranger.

"You remembered your name," he prodded, gut tight. Focus, he had to focus. "You must have remembered Thunder Key."

"I didn't know why I remembered Thunder Key. I just knew it was where I wanted to go. I knew my name was Leah because of the bracelet. That's all. I didn't know my last name."

"Where did you get Wells?"

"A road sign." She rubbed her temple as if her head ached. "That night—it was like a nightmare. Just another nightmare. Sometimes it's hard to know how much of it was real. I remember the rain, and being so frightened."

"I know this is hard, Leah, but I need you to tell me about your nightmares. Maybe we can put it together, figure it out."

"Do you think I've never tried?" she said, and her voice cracked. "In the beginning, I couldn't help but try because the nightmares came so often." She stopped, caught her breath. He could hear the strain in her voice. "Then I learned to stop them. As much as I could, I stopped the dreams. I had no choice—the panic attacks—I had to get control of them, and the only way was to stop trying to remember."

She stood suddenly, paced away from him. Instinctively he rose, wanting to go after her, comfort her, barely resisting the hellish urge to hold her. He stopped in the middle of the room, watching her desperate form silhouetted against the garden doors.

"You realize you could be wrong, completely wrong, about everything," she said, so low he barely heard. She turned. "Especially about me."

He felt something icy prick at the back of his neck.

"Have you ever considered that maybe I'm not in danger? That maybe someone's looking for me, rifling through my apartment, watching me and photographing me not because they mean me harm but because I've done harm? Maybe I've done something wrong."

"Are you kidding?" he said immediately, still struggling to comprehend where she was going with this. "You fed stray dogs and worked in a soup kitchen, for Christ's sake! It wasn't enough for you to send money to one of those third-world children on the TV charity commercials—you told me we could afford to send enough to help a whole village and so we did. You put your name on a bone-marrow donor list in case you could help save a stranger's life." Now he couldn't help himself. He strode toward her, grabbed hold of her. "The woman I knew wouldn't have hurt anyone."

She locked her tormented eyes on him.

"Then maybe you should be as scared of the truth as I am," she said. "Because if my dreams are telling me what I think they are, I was never the woman you thought you knew. I think I've killed someone."

Chapter 9

Roman shook his head, and to Leah his eyes looked as tortured as she felt. "That's crazy."

"Well, welcome to my world," she said, and pulled away from his haunting hold. "I did something wrong, Roman. Something terrible. If you want to know the truth about me then you'd better be ready to face that possibility. In my dreams I was there, with a dead man. And I'm holding the gun."

His expression was filled with anxiety and she didn't think he believed her. She had no idea how to convince him.

"I can't believe that."

"Why not? I was going somewhere that night, driving down that highway—why wouldn't my husband have known where I was going, what I was doing there?" she pointed out. "I must have had secrets from you."

"Not that kind of secret. The woman I knew wouldn't have hurt a fly."

"In my nightmares I hear a voice. And yesterday that voice was on the phone in Morrie's office."

His eyes didn't move from hers. "That's why you dropped the phone. That's why you had the panic attack."

She felt as if she was choking. She was close to a panic attack right now. Carefully she forced herself to breathe.

"Tell me what you heard," he said.

"'I know who you are. I know what you've done.'" She took a ragged breath. "That was it."

"That doesn't mean you killed someone."

She made a bitter sound in her throat and moved away from him. "You wanted to put it together, well put it together. I had a secret, something terrible I had done. And I ran away. Maybe that's what I was doing that night, running away."

He stalked toward her, closing the distance she desperately needed to create. The spacious bungalow seemed to shrink. The bed stood in the center of the room, mocking her with a past she couldn't remember, and the truth that it wasn't Roman she feared so much as herself. She wanted him, had wanted him from the second she'd laid eyes on him.

"That's a lot of maybes," he said grimly. "But you can't go on living like this, thinking you did something like that. We have to find the truth."

Leah swallowed hard. He thought if they found the truth, it would exonerate her. And she was overwhelmed by the realization that she didn't want to disappoint this man.

And a dreadful certainty that she was going to. Was that why she'd run away that night, to save him from the truth about her? If she was right, they could both be in for more heartache than she could even imagine right now.

He strode away, picked up the phone on the bedside table, punched in a series of numbers. She took a seat again, her legs suddenly weak.

"Mark?" he said, his voice clipped, businesslike. It was like having a glimpse into his professional life in New York. This was Roman, the man in charge. It was eerily familiar, and the sensation rocked her mind. "I need your help," he continued. "I need the name of a doctor in Miami. A psychiatrist."

His back was to Leah now.

"I can't discuss it. And again, please," he added, "don't mention this to Gen, or anyone in the family. I'm counting on you, Mark."

Mark. The name meant nothing to Leah.

Roman hung up the phone.

"Who is Mark?" she asked.

"My brother-in-law. He's a physician. He's married to my sister, Gen. Genevieve."

She was reminded with a shock of what Morrie had told her about the Bradshaw dynasty. How in the hell had she ever fit into that? "Do they know—about me, that you've found me?"

"Mark knows, but he thinks I've lost it down here." His voice was dry. "He probably thinks the psychiatrist should be for me. My whole family is pretty sure I've lost my mind since I left New York."

"That doesn't bother you?"

He smiled for just a moment, and she remembered

how dangerously sexy he could be. "I don't care what anyone thinks anymore, Leah." He came toward her in the quiet light of the bungalow. She felt her heart beat faster. "Mark's going to call back with a reference. That's all that matters. I want to be sure you see someone good. I wouldn't know where to start. Mark should be able to give me a good name."

Leah sat there for a long beat. She felt stunned, as if a bomb had exploded in her world. She didn't know what to think, what to do. There was too much to take in.

She needed to pull herself together, and she couldn't do it here.

"I need to go to work," she said after a long beat. She needed to not be alone with Roman. "We'll be opening soon. Just because I'm staying here, that doesn't mean I can't go to work." Surely he hadn't meant that. They'd be surrounded by people at the bar all day. "I need to keep busy."

He nodded, and intense relief soaked her that he wasn't going to argue that point. But when the day was over, they'd come back here to this bungalow where she would be alone with a man she didn't know and desperately wanted at the same time.

What then?

Roman called the Thunder Key Police Department from the Shark and Fin. And got a recording. There was a number for emergencies, and he tried that one, only to be told by the woman who answered that a possible break-in where nothing had been stolen was not an emergency but that they'd send an officer around to the bar as soon as possible. Unfortunately, tomorrow was as soon as possible.

Roman would have liked to reach through the phone line and strangle the woman. "I think someone is watching her, possibly stalking her," he said tightly.

"Almost all of our officers have been called away to a search on Coral Key," the woman explained. "We can only handle emergencies right now, sir."

He sat at Morrie's desk. *I know who you are. I know what you've done.*

He couldn't believe Leah had killed someone. But she believed it.

What do you know about this girl? his parents had asked, berating him when he'd announced their quick marriage. *She's not one of us. She's not good enough for you.*

Their objections had gone on and on. Walter and Barbara Bradshaw had huge ambitions for their only son. A future in politics had long been at the top of the list of their expectations. Leah with her lack of prestigious family background and carefree-artist temperament had not fit the bill they'd had in mind for their son's wife. They'd made noises at the time about having Leah's history checked and Roman had responded with a resounding refusal.

He picked up the phone, punched in the number to Bradshaw Securities. "Walter Bradshaw," he said to the secretary. "Tell him it's Roman."

His father picked up a moment later. "Roman. Where are you?"

"I'm still in Thunder Key. Look," he went on, before his father could launch into all the reasons he should come back to New York, "I want to know if you had Leah investigated."

"What?"

"When we married. You wanted to have her investigated then."

"You got quite upset about it, if you'll recall," his father said.

"Did that stop you?" Roman asked.

The line was silent. "Son, I have a meeting."

"Did that stop you?"

He could feel the tension in the phone line all the way from New York to Florida.

"If you found out something about Leah, anything at all, I need you to tell me."

"Son, she's dead. It doesn't matter now."

At least now he knew Mark had kept his promise not to tell his family about Leah. "It matters. I want to know."

"We had her investigated. We didn't find out anything."

Roman felt as if all the air went out of his chest. He should have known, all along, that his parents had investigated Leah despite their assurances to leave her alone. But now, ironically, it was exactly the information he needed.

But what did that mean about Leah's dreams?

"Son, what's going on down there? We're worried about you."

"I'm fine. Stop worrying." Roman said goodbye and hung up the phone. He turned over possibilities in his mind. Leah was convinced there was something terrible in her past. But maybe her dreams were just that—dreams. Horrible nightmares. Random crimes were reported on the news all the time. Sometimes not so random. Strangers who followed women in mall parking lots, broke into their homes. Men who became obsessed for some reason or another.

The idea didn't do anything to make him feel better. Either way, Leah was in danger.

Leah put together a small bag of things from her apartment. Roman waited for her at the door with his hot blue eyes and finger-raked brown hair. His casual jeans and T-shirt hugged his killer body.

She walked outside with him into the clear, dark night. They'd driven to the bar earlier in Roman's rental car, and he opened the passenger side door for her, stowing her bag in the back. Flicking on the headlights, he maneuvered down the narrow road back toward the hotel. Leah lowered her window a crack.

She leaned against the seat, breathed in the fresh night air and tried very hard not to think about how strangely familiar it felt to be so near Roman.

"This could be completely unnecessary," she said, looking at him. "We haven't seen that man again. His presence could have been unconnected to my past. The phone call yesterday could have been a prank." She was trying to convince herself, but she felt chilled in the warm, heavy night even as she spoke.

"I was freaking out every time the phone even rang yesterday," she went on. "Maybe I didn't hear those words at all. Maybe—" She turned her head away from him, stared into the misty darkness of the wooded night. "Maybe I imagined them."

"'Maybe' isn't good enough." He came to a stop sign.

Reaching over, he touched her chin gently, forcing her to look back at him. She was ultraaware of the strong warmth of his fingers.

In that moment, in the dark of the car, they could have been the only living humans left on the planet.

"I know that you're frightened," he said. "But you don't have to be frightened of me." A long pause, and he didn't take his eyes off hers. "Are you frightened of me, Leah?"

The answer to his question was elusive, tangled in the web of her lost memories and her present confusion. She didn't know what to say.

"I just hate for you to have to play my baby-sitter," she finally managed to tell him, avoiding a direct reply.

He looked at her for a very long beat, and something inside his soulful eyes made her quiver somewhere very deep within her body.

"Trust me," he said, "I don't feel like your baby-sitter."

In that fleeting instant, she thought she saw the same impenetrable emotions in his eyes that tangled within her heart. Pain, loneliness, desire...

He turned his attention back to the road. Leah hugged her arms to herself in the dark car.

"Bathroom's in there," he said, pointing the way once they were inside the bungalow at the White Seas. "Feel free to make yourself at home."

She shut the door, grateful to be alone. The bungalow's bathroom was blatantly luxurious. Gold fixtures, marble spa tub, separate shower built for two. Had they shared that shower, that spa tub, on their honeymoon?

They'd been husband and wife. He'd grieved for her
when he thought she was dead. But how did he feel
about her now? He had pointedly not made any avow-
als of love to her, and aside from that one kiss, he'd
barely touched her.

She pushed away the thoughts, dropped her bag on
the floor of the bathroom and turned on the faucet in
the sink. What had she done? Where had she been
driving that night? She splashed cold water on her
face. The questions were killing her. She wanted them
to stop, but they just kept coming.

Her cut hand burned beneath the bandage as she
dried her face, reminding her to take her antibiotic.
She still didn't want to take any of the pain pills.

She'd brought a pair of pajamas with her—light-
weight, the top buttoned, the bottoms long. But even
covered as prudishly as that, she felt embarrassed to
come out of the bathroom. The situation was undeniably intimate and strange.

Roman sat at the table in the bungalow, a glass containing pale-gold liquid in his hand. His long legs were
stretched out to the side.

"Wine?" he offered.

She nodded, still standing just outside the bathroom.
The bungalow lay shrouded in shadows, only one
lamp spilling a low glow across the large room.

He'd already placed another glass on the table.
There was a small bar in the bungalow that included
several bottles and carafes. He poured her wine. In the
quiet of the bungalow, the smooth plop of the liquid
sounded loud. She sat across from him, took the glass,
briefly brushing his fingers as he released it into her

hand. He smelled musky, male, dangerous and safe all at once.

A pang of longing speared through her. Her life could be in danger and yet she was punishingly aware of this man. *You feel this connection between us.* Yes, she felt it.

And it was nearly unbearable.

Roman took another sip from his glass, watching her intently. Her heart drummed wildly against the wall of her chest. How was she going to spend the night in the same room with him when her entire being came to aching life just from his proximity?

If she gave in to those feelings, she didn't know if she could handle it, keep her perspective. Keep things from going too far. The bed was like a living, breathing thing behind her.

A sharp knock sounded on the door, and Leah jerked, spilling wine on the burnished surface of the table. She grabbed a napkin from the holder on the shelf, mopped up her mess.

"It's room service, Leah," Roman explained. "I ordered some food. I know you haven't eaten all day."

"I'm just jumpy. I swear I'm not usually this much of a klutz."

"I know," he said.

His eyes made her feel even more nervous. Yes, he did know. He knew better than she did what she was like, didn't he?

But he didn't know everything. He didn't know where she'd been going that night. He didn't know her secrets.

And she didn't know his. There'd been something

wrong with their marriage. How could she know he'd told her the full truth?

He went to the door. A short, uniformed waiter entered with a tray of covered dishes.

"Just set it on the table." After Roman let the waiter back out and shut the door, securing it with the inside lock, he said, "I'm sorry I didn't wait for you to come out of the bathroom to order, but I figured you were hungry. I ordered some of your favorites."

Leah swallowed thickly. He knew her favorites.

She took another sip of the wine.

He lifted the covers off the dishes to reveal skewered shrimp with steamed vegetables and rice. The rich grilled aroma had her mouth watering immediately. She *was* hungry, and he was right, she hadn't eaten all day. Her stomach had been in turmoil, her heart in her throat. And now?

Her stomach was still in turmoil, her heart was still in her throat. But she was starved and eating was better than sitting here wondering what to talk about with a stranger who had been her lover.

Using a fork, she slid a piece of seared shrimp off the skewer and popped it in her mouth.

"Let's go over your normal routine in Thunder Key," Roman said after a minute.

"I don't think anyone here in Thunder Key wants to hurt me," she said automatically.

"We don't know that. While it looks as if this has something to do with your past, we could be wrong. It could be a stranger who has developed an obsession about you. Or if it is someone from your past, it could be someone who is already here, someone you come into daily contact with and don't even realize you know. They could have some connection to the man watching you. We just don't know at this point.''

"You don't recognize anyone in Thunder Key, do you?'' she asked him.

"No," he said grimly, "but I only knew your friends in New York. They were mostly people from your design studio.''

Leah didn't want to think that one of the friends she'd made in Thunder Key could be connected with her past and with the man watching her. Everyone in Thunder Key had been wonderful to her. The idea of a stranger being obsessed with her wasn't any more comfortable, though.

"We have to rule out anyone here being involved,'' he added. "Whether it's a stranger or a friend.''

"You're not a policeman.''

He looked frustrated. "Well, so far we're not getting a heck of a lot of help from the cops here. An officer is supposed to come by the bar tomorrow— there was some kind of search going on involving another Key today. I know it sounds like I'm reaching,'' Roman went on, "but I want a list of the people you've been acquainted with since you came to Thunder Key.''

Roman took notes while she spoke. Her close friends were few—Joey, Viv, Marian, Morrie. She was acquainted with numerous residents on the small island, however, due to her work at the Shark and Fin.

"You run in the mornings,'' he filled in. "Once a week you work at the shop in Smugglers Village. You go to the coffeehouse, the library, the grocery store. Am I missing anything? Do you go to the other islands much?''

Leah swallowed hard. "How do you know all that? Oh, my God, *you* were watching me."

"I couldn't believe it was you," he admitted. "I watched you for days before I could bring myself to speak to you. I was afraid—" He was silent for a beat. "I was afraid you'd disappear, the way you did in my dreams."

He'd dreamed about her. He'd dreamed of losing her. It was awful, and she didn't know what to say. She just knew they were both hurting.

She answered his question. "I go to the fabric studio in Key West." She gave him the name.

"What do you know about Morrie?"

Leah hesitated. Morrie had been too good a friend to her for her to feel comfortable discussing the shadier side of his past.

"I need the truth, Leah."

"Morrie has a criminal history," she said reluctantly. "But he's been nothing but kind to me."

"What sort of criminal history?"

"I don't know the details. He was in prison. That's all in the past, though. He's trying to work things out with his family now. That's why he wants to sell the Shark and Fin—so he can move to New Mexico."

"What about any other staff at the bar? Has there been any trouble in the past eighteen months? Anyone who could have something against you?"

"I don't think so. I fired a girl right after Morrie left, but she wasn't coming in to work, so I don't think it could be related. I had to replace her. She was a no-show half the time. Morrie'd given her a lot of chances and he'd given me the go-ahead to let her go if the problems kept up. I hated to do it but we needed someone more dependable. There's nothing any of these people I've come into contact with in Thunder Key have ever said or done to make me believe I knew them in the past except—''

Roman's gaze locked on hers.

''Except who?''

''You,'' she admitted softly. Her stomach fluttered, and she looked down at her plate.

''I'm glad, Leah.'' His hard voice filled with kindness, caring, and that just about broke her will to resist him. She looked up, captured by the pull of her name on his lips. ''I want you to remember me.''

''You want me to remember what a bastard you were?'' she said, purposefully baiting him in order to wedge any distance she could between them.

Something shifted in his eyes. As difficult as the past eighteen months had been for her, they couldn't have been easy for him, either.

''I'm sorry,'' she said. ''You didn't deserve that.''

Now she felt like a heel. He didn't ask any more questions. They finished their meal, and they took turns brushing their teeth—an oddly intimate routine with a man who felt like a stranger. When she came out, she found Roman had opened the bungalow's entertainment center. He'd turned off the light, leaving the glow of the television screen to light the room. Leah sat down on the floor at the foot of the bed. She noticed Roman had piled pillows there. It was as close to the bed as she could bring herself to get.

She hunched her knees, placing her arms around her legs, and leaned back into the pillows. Roman surfed channels, finally stopping on a grainy black-and-white movie. He sat beside her on the floor, giving her plenty of distance and not nearly enough at the same time.

The film had to have been from the forties. It was horribly acted, terribly stiff and ridiculous.

She realized he was watching her, not the movie. She looked at him, pulled away from the B movie by his excruciatingly intense eyes.

"Do you remember that you loved movies like this?" he asked.

She blinked. "Are you serious? The aliens look like they're wrapped in tinfoil, and did they have a five-year-old in charge of special effects? Are you telling me I had the worst taste in the world in movies?"

Roman laughed, showing those damn dimples and making her heart beat too fast. "You loved old movies, especially science fiction," he told her. "The worse the movie, the more you liked it. And you always made me watch them with you."

"Maybe I was just punishing you for being a bastard," she said jokingly, trying to keep the conversation from getting too serious.

"Old movies made you laugh," Roman said. "You loved to laugh."

The way he said it, so tenderly, so romantically, had the breath clogging in her throat. It was getting harder and harder to think of him as a stranger, as someone she didn't dare completely trust.

"I hated the movies," he continued softly.

"So why did you watch them with me?"

He was quiet for a beat. The light from the TV flickered across his rugged features. "I loved to watch you laugh."

Her stomach dipped inside her and she knew she

couldn't handle where this conversation could be going.

"I'm tired," she said suddenly. "I hardly slept last night. I think it would be better if I just went to bed."

He watched her. "All right, Leah." He picked up the remote and flicked the TV off. It took a second for her eyes to adjust to the dark. She realized he was heading for the chaise in the corner. He'd taken a couple pillows from the floor.

"No." She was having a heart attack thinking about getting in that bed. She almost wanted to tell him to turn the movie back on. But the movie hadn't been such a good idea, either. "Let me take the chaise. This is your bungalow."

"You need a good night's sleep," he countered.

She was left with no choice. She climbed into the huge, romantically shrouded bed, almost sure she'd have an impossible time falling to sleep. She shut her eyes and worked not to notice that the fresh scent of the clean sheets still somehow carried the musky male scent that was undeniably Roman.

Her nipples ached in the darkness and she could have sworn she could hear his heartbeat across the room. She didn't know how long it took her to fall asleep. She only knew that sometime in the night, she drifted off into a place that was as familiar as it was foreign.

She felt herself dancing across an apartment floor, laughing, falling into the lap of a man who growled and kissed her, flinging her back against the sofa. He planted himself over her, suckling at her earlobes, kissing her neck, enticing her, making love to her. They ripped their clothes off, eager and passionate.

Reaching up to the faceless man she'd kissed so many times in her dreams, his features cleared, focused for the first time. And it was Roman she held, Roman she kissed.

Then Roman was gone, his face transposed into a blur of a man in a white coat. She was on a sidewalk, buildings soaring around her, running, running, and every time she looked back, the man in the white coat was following her. Terrified, she stumbled on a crack in the pavement, fell. The only sound she knew was the pounding of his feet, closer and closer.

Leah sat bolt upright in the bed, darkness surrounding her. She didn't know how long it was before she realized she was screaming.

Chapter 10

"Leah!" Roman gripped Leah's arms against the pillows over her head, trying everything to still her crazed thrashing. She'd slugged his face once already before he'd pinned her back on the bed. If he didn't have a black-and-blue eye tomorrow, he'd be lucky.

Now she kicked him, struggling beneath the fine-spun sheet. She'd already thrown all the other covers off.

He risked letting go of one arm to take hold of her thrashing face, force her to focus on him. "Leah, it's me, Roman. You don't have to be afraid. You're not alone. You're safe. You're with me."

In the shadowed bed, he could see her tormented eyes shining up at him, raw and wild. Long heartbeats passed, the only sound in the room now her too-fast breaths. He shifted slightly, meaning to take his weight off her, slide down next to her, but she must have thought he was leaving because she gripped his shoulders, pulled at him. She was clinging to him.

"I'm just—" he began, his voice filling with rough emotion. He took a breath, struggled for control. "I'm not going anywhere." He lowered his body beside her, the sheet and her pajamas and the briefs and T-shirt he'd stripped down to in the dark when he'd gone to bed on the chaise the only barrier between them. Through the thin sheet, he felt her every pulse, every breath. Her skin felt hot, clammy, but she shivered in his arms.

The sweet agony of holding her this way was nearly unbearable. He was dying holding her, and he realized they were both trembling—he as much as her. He couldn't help himself. He put his arms around her, pulled her closer, touching her shoulders, her hair, her face.

"You were there, in my dream," she said suddenly.

"I'm here now," he said. "And nobody's going to hurt you ever again."

"I want the dreams to go away. I want them to stop."

He wanted to tell her he could make them stop, and he'd never felt so inadequate in his life. All he could think was that he never wanted to let her go. He wanted to tell her that somehow, if he just held her long enough, he could make all her bad dreams go away.

But it wasn't true and they both knew it. So he just held her and said nothing. He felt the wetness of her tears against his shoulder. The scent of her filled him, teasing and torturing him with her nearness.

And he'd thought sleeping across the room from her had been difficult.

"You were the only good part of my dream," she whispered, her voice stark.

Oh, God. His heart ached. She gazed up at him like a lost fairy in the liquid night, her lambent eyes shining with need and despair. He didn't know what to say, what to do, and then she said something he knew she only would have said in that midnight bed.

"Don't leave me alone."

The pain in her voice grabbed him by the throat. "I won't," he swore to her.

She moved, shifting slightly to slide her arms around his neck. His muscles tensed from the onslaught of desire. He was linked—heart, mind and soul—to this lost fairy-wife of his in a way he'd never been linked to anyone in his life before. She had been the one person who had made him whole, lifted him out of his cold, sterile business world, but she was someone else now, not that same ray of lightness that had once graced his life. She had her secrets, and he had his, and if he were a wiser man, he would tread carefully. He would get out of this bed before he did something they might both regret in the morning.

But he didn't feel wise tonight.

"I'll stay here with you all night," he said. "If that's what you want." He skimmed his hand up along her shadowed jaw, and she leaned into his touch, closing her eyes.

"I want—" she whispered, then stopped.

"What do you want, Leah?" he coaxed her.

She opened her eyes. And he dared to believe he saw the same bond in her gaze that he felt in his heart.

The same aching, desperate desire. It was an intuitive, subliminal connection that went beyond memories. It was in skin on skin, touch on touch, gaze on gaze.

"I want to know what it felt like to be your wife," she said softly, her words rushing over his heart in one tender tidal wave. "For just one night. Even if that's all we have. I want the one good thing I dreamed. The dream I dreamed of you."

He was drowning in her. "What did you dream of me?"

Their faces were only inches apart. He could almost hear her heart pounding, as violently as his own.

"I dreamed," she whispered, "that we made love."

Roman had no words. He was beyond amazed, beyond lost. She was everything he wanted, and she was offering herself to him. So many feelings—guilt, need, desire, pain—tangled together, threatening to spin him out of control.

"I have to know that *one* thing in my mind, in my heart, in my dreams, is real, and that it's something beautiful," she said. "Make love to me. Show me that it's real."

"Leah," he started, overwhelmed. "Of course it's real." Sweet Lord, this was all he'd wanted to hear her say, but it was so dangerous. That wiser man sitting on his shoulder told him it wasn't too late to back away.

But she clung to him and he had no idea if she was clinging to a dream or to a man. He knew he couldn't bear it if he woke up tomorrow and she was sorry for what she'd said tonight.

And he also knew there was no way he was going to be able to stop now. It was too late. Way too late.

Tomorrow was far away from this night-shrouded bed.

He had his wife back. For one night. Even if all she was reaching for was a dream, a sweet solace from her pain and fear, he was the one in her arms. And God help him, he couldn't resist her. He'd promised her he wouldn't do this very thing, but it was she who was begging him to break that promise.

And so he kissed her with all the passion that had been sealed up inside him for eighteen months. She kissed him back, and he tasted the salty flavor of her tears along with the sweet tang of her lips. He kissed her face, her neck, her ears, his hands roaming over her, and all the while she drew him tight with her arms. He couldn't get enough of her and he never wanted this night to end.

She smelled like bougainvilleas and sweet memories.

"I want to remember you," she whispered against his lips. "Make me remember."

His heart swelled and emotion stung his eyes. He kissed her again with heated energy as his hands reacquainted themselves with her body. He wanted to be so tender and careful with her, but he was driven by a force beyond his power as a soft groan sounded in her throat. Through the thin material of her pajamas he felt her slender body, and he knew no past, no future, only Leah, here and now, in his arms.

Her hands streaked over his back, her need matching his own. Desperate now, burning, he laid her back on the pillows and turned his questing attention to her body, one by one slowly tearing apart the buttons of her pajama top.

If tonight did turn out to be all they had, he was going to make it last.

The top came apart, revealing her night-kissed breasts. They were small, perfect, and he longed for them. "Do you remember this?" he asked in a hushed voice, claiming one as his again with an excruciatingly tender mouth. "And this?" he asked again, suckling the other tight nub.

Her answer was a moan, and she dug her fingers into his hair, then he realized she was tugging at his shirt. He sat back, pulled it over his head. She reached up with searching hands and placed one over his heart, as if feeling it beat.

He took a moment then to gaze down at her in the shrouded shadows. Moonlight grazed through the mosquito netting, giving him a dreamy view of her silken torso. But it was her eyes that drew him, all darkness and hunger. He was on fire for her, and she was everything to him. She was his heart. He pressed hot kisses to her face, his blood pounding, emotion filling him for this intimacy that was so familiar and yet new at the same time. Too new for words.

It was simpler to show her how right and real their love could be. And so he did, capturing her mouth again with sweet fury. Then he laved a tormenting line of kisses down her stomach, his hands skimming over the sheer material of her clothing. But that wasn't enough for her, and she pushed at her pajama bottoms, ripping away the twisted sheet. He pulled away the pajamas, leaving only the ephemeral covering of her underwear.

"Leah," he breathed harshly. "Leah—" He would just die if she stopped him now.

"Touch me." She seduced him with her breathy wonder. "Touch me and don't stop."

And no longer did he even hear the whisper of the wiser man who would have left this bed long ago. There was no chance in hell he would regret this night, even if she did. She was pleading with him to continue, and a team of wild horses couldn't have dragged him away.

He slid one hand inside her panties, his shaking fingers meeting her hot, wet center. Slow, he wanted to take this so slow. But sweet heaven above, he was so lost.

In her dreams it had never been this good. Leah felt her body tremble as Roman's fingers coaxed her heated core to life. This was madness; she knew it on some faraway level. But it was an exquisite insanity that she needed in the same way she needed air to breathe.

The need she felt for this stranger-husband of hers was almost painfully intense. She felt as if she were blind, feeling for memory by touch, by her fingers on his hard, incredible chest and shoulders and back.

Then, as his fingers slipped higher inside her, it was a different sort of madness altogether that she experienced. She was hungry and desperate and so eager to let this mindless passion, this all-encompassing physical sensation, take her over. She wanted to be free, for this one night, of fear and hurt and dread. And his lips, his hands, his heated body was her salvation.

Somewhere deep within her heart, she knew he had always been her salvation. The familiarity of losing herself in his tender lovemaking brought an aching recognition. There had to have been more to their marriage than this passion, but whatever it was, she didn't want to know it tonight.

Fumbling, she tore apart the waist of his briefs. He gazed down at her with something wild in his eyes, something heartbreakingly needy, and her stomach dropped away. He kissed her with heated lingering, then pulled away to slide off his briefs. He was back in an instant, his hard body bare and unbelievable. She had a glimpse of powerful, corded muscle and gleaming moon-starred skin. He was man, all man, and she felt all woman beneath his gaze. And heavy—she felt so heavy everywhere. She couldn't have moved from this bed if elephants had suddenly stampeded into the bungalow.

"Remember me here," he said, laying his long, hard body against her. "And here," he added as he smoothed away her panties with a flick of his strong hand. "And here." He claimed her mouth in a soul-searing frenzy of a kiss that swept her away from the bungalow. She didn't know where she was anymore, and it didn't matter. She was in his arms. That was all she knew.

She was acutely aware of him sliding his hand between them, cupping her breast possessively then dipping lower, to the core of need burning for his touch again.

"Leah." He slipped inside again, and she was already aching and hot and damp for him. "Remember me here, Leah."

He flicked his fingertip against a hidden nub she hadn't even realized existed. She whimpered and moaned against his mouth. He kissed her again, even as he explored the secret cleft of her femininity, lighting erotic fires inside her body. Then sharply, unexpectedly, a fireburst rocketed through her, and she dug her nails into his back, riding the tumultuous storm of his touch and her response, then coming back to some slow free fall only to find he was doing it again. And again, as if he couldn't get enough of her.

And she couldn't get enough of him, this stranger-husband who felt like home in her arms. She explored back with restless fingers, moving from his back to his buttocks and then to the steel-hard heat that told her just how much he wanted her. Then she wrapped her legs around him, instinctively, and guided that hot length of him into her, no longer satisfied with mere fingers.

His mouth fused to hers as he rocked with her, and she gripped him for dear life, hanging on by the one sensual thread of his kiss. Every breath now was a whimper, a little cry, each rhythmic rock taking her higher, and he with her. Inside her, the burning ache quivered and spilled over again. She breathed his name against his mouth and he breathed hers back.

"Oh, Roman," she gasped, and clutched his shoulders as another shudder took her away, shattered her into splintering pieces of pure pleasure.

"Leah, sweetheart," he groaned, and she was vaguely aware of him collapsing, damp and spent, over her, then carefully shifting his weight from her. He lay back on the bed, breathing as hard as she. The scent of him, musk and mint and lost need, both comforted her and shocked her with its familiarity.

She felt so right here in his arms.

He was the first to move, pressing gentle kisses against her face, her neck, and all that she couldn't remember and didn't know fell away. She settled into the crook of his strong shoulder, and when she dreamed, it was only of him, and for once she dreaded waking more than sleeping.

Light filtered through the terrace sheers, painting the bungalow with dawn fingers. Leah opened her eyes, dazed for a long beat. She wasn't alone.

She was in Roman's bungalow. Roman's bed.

He lay with one arm sprawled over her. There was a slightly purplish shadow beneath one eye. The events of the day before—and of the night—crashed over her, and she recalled how she'd come to be here in his bungalow.

Oh, God, she had made love with him. In the surreal cocoon only darkness could create, she had yielded to what she had longed to do since she'd laid eyes on him that first day in the bar. Danger, railroad-crossing bars, stop signs had all been forgotten, swept away. She had used his arms, his lovemaking, to blot out her fears.

The pieces of her nightmare lay in puzzlelike fashion in her mind. Mixed up with the dream of making love to this stranger, the picture they were meant to form was lost in the shrouded mist of the night, familiar and yet mysterious, beautiful and horrible at one time.

She remembered Roman holding her, comforting her. Making love to her. Gazing at his sculpted face, she realized with a little shock that she'd hit him. She had caused that bruise beneath his eye. And he had been so gentle with her. But he could be fierce, too. His lovemaking had been that of a man long denied and possessive. What manner of man was this husband of hers? Hard and tender, open yet enigmatic.

Safe and dangerous.

As she watched he opened his eyes, and he stared at her for a very long time. She saw the memory of their lovemaking in his glimmer-blue depths. "Good morning, Leah," he finally said.

And it felt so right, so familiar, it bladed a tight keening of loss into her chest.

"Your eye," she said, unable to deal with the emotion inside her. "I'm sorry."

"I'm not sorry about anything that happened last night, Leah."

Their gazes held.

She thought of what a fragile facade it was, the two of them together in this honeymoon bed. It was so perfect, she could almost believe it would last forever. But it wasn't possible. She had no memory, no idea of her past, who she truly was beyond Roman's wife.

And that truth, when she found it, could destroy everything.

"This isn't fair to you," she began. "To you, I'm your wife, to me, you're—"

"A stranger," he finished for her.

She didn't know what to say.

"I'm a big boy, Leah," Roman said quietly. "I'm not expecting anything from you. Last night…was last night." He reached up, touched her cheek briefly. "Don't tell me you're sorry. Just let it be what it was—something we both wanted, needed."

His words, his gaze, were so direct, and yet a shield

all at the same time. He was protecting himself and her. How would he feel when he knew the truth, whatever it turned out to be? He couldn't know and neither could she.

The emotions building within her, long hidden even from herself these past eighteen months, were surfacing, out of her control. The more time she spent with Roman, the more of those emotions could come out. And if last night had been a mistake, the more hurt both of them could be when it was all over.

"This is so complicated." Her soft voice sounded bleak to her own ears in the quiet bungalow. *I don't even know who you are and already I don't want to lose you,* she wanted to say. But she couldn't. She didn't dare.

"Only if we make it that way," he said, his eyes shuttered.

The palm fronds rustled in the morning breeze outside the terrace. She sat up, fumbling for the sheet with cold, clumsy fingers despite the warmth around her.

"There was something new in my dreams last night," she said. Even her nightmares were easier to talk about than her feelings of what had happened between them in the darkness.

His gaze sharpened. He lay there against the bed, unshaven, excruciatingly handsome, watching her. How many times had she seen him this same way?

Concentrate. It was so hard to focus when she was in this bed with him, remembering how his hands had felt on her skin, awakening her body to…

To things she had no business thinking about. Not now.

"I was in a city," she said carefully, marshalling

her train of thought. "There were tall buildings, long streets—"

"New York?"

"I don't know." She hesitated, trying to bring back more details. "I was being chased, and I fell."

"Who was chasing you?"

"All I remember is that he wore a white coat with some kind of insignia on it, like his name, but I didn't read a name in my dream. Like a doctor or laboratory coat. Or a pet groomer, for all I know."

She chewed her lip, adjusting the sheet to keep her body hidden in this bare morning light. Last night in the darkness had been one thing. In the day she felt modest, strange about her nakedness. She saw a shadow cross his eyes. He noticed her shyness. Did it hurt him that the wife he knew so well was so uncomfortable in her nudity before him?

There was no way for her to know. He was far too skilled at quickly cloaking his feelings from her view.

"If something did happen in my past," she continued. "If I did do something wrong, maybe I was sent to doctors, hospitals, I don't know." She shuddered at the prospect that she might have been in a mental institution at one time. The not knowing just got worse all the time as more and more possibilities occurred to her. "Maybe it's why I have this fear of seeing a doctor now."

"If you were in trouble and had been seen by a doctor, he would hardly have been chasing you down a city street," Roman pointed out.

"It was a nightmare. I could have things mixed up. A few months ago I dreamed I was carrying out plates of seashells to customers. When I woke up, I realized

I'd forgotten to put in an order I was supposed to put in with one of our suppliers. Dreams aren't literal—they're more like phantoms of our fears. I'm afraid of men in little white coats. That can't be good.''

She tried to laugh as if she could make light of it, but the sound she made came out more like a choked hiccup.

"Hey," he said. "We don't know that yet, okay? Remember that."

She remembered it all too well.

Then he got out of the bed and she realized he was naked, too. Her gaze zeroed in on his muscular buttocks. She felt a quivery panic-desire in her belly, and she watched him as he walked across the floor. He made absolutely no attempt to cover himself. And she made no attempt to stop looking at him, to her own shock.

Despite her modesty about her own body, she was, oh my, shameless about his—and she'd been equally shameless in the way she'd responded to him sexually last night. She *loved* sex, and she loved having it with *this* man. It was a dangerous revelation. It was pure insanity that all she wanted was for him to come back to the bed...and her.

Yep, she was ready for the men in little white coats. She wanted to stay at the White Seas all day and have sex with her stranger-husband despite all the reasons why that would be wrong.

At the door of the bathroom, he turned back and caught her watching him.

Chapter 11

The sea rolled lazily through the Shark and Fin's plateglass windows. A deep blue gray formed on the horizon. A storm was brewing somewhere out in the Atlantic, breaking the bright morning into shades of light and dark. Roman watched Leah move around the bar, her expression subdued, pensive as she went about her routine filling napkin dispensers and laying bar shakers on the counter.

She'd had a grueling few days. She was obviously not okay today. And neither was he. He felt shaken and torn up inside. But he was more worried about her, about the pressure she was under. The nightmares, the fears, it was like a noose tightening around her.

He unloaded a box of bar straws into a container. It was early yet, and none of the other staff had arrived.

"Are you serious about buying the bar?" Leah

asked suddenly. "Or was that all a ruse, to get close to me?"

"It's real," Roman said, amazed at the fact that it *was* real as he spoke the words. He'd come up with the notion of purchasing the business merely to spend time with her, but somehow in the days that had passed he'd realized that he wanted to own the Shark and Fin. It fit perfectly into the way he wanted to live now and in the future. And he wanted Leah by his side. "You always said we could be happy here in the Keys, running a bar. You were right."

"Don't buy it because of me."

"I have no desire to go back to my life in New York," he told her. "That was the life of a different man."

She watched him, her eyes tense, exhausted. Did she believe him? Despite how freely she'd given her body to him last night, her mind was still far away, secret, shielded from him.

"Leah, take the day off."

She put down the last bar shaker and looked at him. "What?"

"You're tired, and you have a right to be. You're going to end up sick if you keep pushing yourself."

"Morrie—"

"Would want you to take the day off if he cares about you like you say he does."

"I can't leave Joey shorthanded."

"Call in extra staff."

She was running out of excuses and he had no intention of letting her off the hook. The phone rang, and she startled. Roman went to grab it but she got to it first. "Shark and Fin."

Still so damn independent. But it was plain she was on edge, big-time.

"I'm sorry, Viv. I know I haven't been in for two days. I'm fine. Just…busy." Leah was silent for a beat. "I was wondering," she said then. Roman saw her turn, gaze out the windows at the undulating sea. "I haven't listened to the news today. I was just about to turn on the TV in the bar. Thanks."

"What was that about?" Roman asked when she hung up.

"Tropical storm on the way," she said. "We could be evacuating in a few days if it keeps its course. Just part of life in the Keys."

Roman imagined how the traffic would tie up in that case, with one highway leading to Miami. "I bet that's a mess."

"If it turns into a hurricane, we'll have plenty of warning. Usually storms slow down or miss us."

He thought of the story she'd told him about the Keys residents who'd died trapped in that lighthouse. He felt a fierce rush of protectiveness and wanted to do something, take Leah away *now*. But she was right, the storm would more than likely pass the Keys by. They'd have to wait and see. It was just one more thing that was out of his control.

Like the storm itself, he couldn't control what was happening to Leah. He could only follow it through to whatever end fate held in store, protect her as best he could. But hadn't the calculating businessman who controlled every aspect of his life always been lost with Leah? She had been like a beam of sunshine he could never quite catch.

Nothing had changed.

He hated the feeling of helplessness, the not knowing. At least he could track a storm.

There was a set over the bar and Leah picked up the remote, flicked it on. She surfed to the cable network that specialized in weather.

Picking up the phone, Roman punched in Mark's number at the hospital while he listened to the weather anchor.

"A new line of strong storms is developing in the Atlantic. Upper winds don't favor rapid development at this time, however, the disturbance has the potential to build in the next forty-eight to seventy-two hours."

Leah leaned on the bar, focused on the screen. Roman worked his way through two receptionists and a nurse before connecting to the floor where Mark was making rounds.

The announcer's voice continued: "Air Force Reserve reconnaissance aircraft are currently en route to investigate this system and updates will—"

"Hey, bud," Mark said. "How's it going down there in the Keys? Sun, sand, no work. Man, are you sure you're not having a midlife crisis down there?"

Roman felt a knot of irritation at Mark's blithe questions. Mark knew he wasn't down here taking a vacation. He knew he was here with Leah. But he didn't believe him. He thought Roman was nuts. "You got a name for me?"

"Sorry I didn't get back to you yesterday, but some of us are still working," Mark said, his tone turning curt. "Look, I know you think you've seen Leah down there, but it's not possible, Roman. She's dead. And if she's not—what the hell is she doing down there? Why didn't she come back to you? You've got to be careful, Roman. More careful than you were in the first place.''

Roman knew what Mark was referring to. He was talking about their marriage, how fast it had all happened. Mark had never accepted Leah any more than the rest of the family had, but in addition, he'd been Nikki Bates's doctor. Leah had blamed him for prescribing the medication Nikki had used to kill herself, which had only increased the conflict in Roman's family over his marriage.

"I just need the name, Mark. Or if that's too much trouble, I'll get out the phone book. But I really want to deal with the best. So if you don't mind—''

"What did you ever know about that girl?'' Mark asked.

Roman felt the knot tighten in his gut. *That girl.*

Leah watched him, her eyes sharp, haunted.

"Either give me the name, or I'm getting off the phone.''

"Fine,'' Mark said. "It's your funeral. Kent Thompson. He's a top-notch psychiatrist out of Miami.'' Mark gave him the number. Roman scratched it down. "Gen's worried about you.''

"Tell her she doesn't need to be. I'm fine. Did you tell her about any of this?''

"No, you asked me not to.''

"Thanks for the name, Mark.'' He hung up before his brother-in-law could ask any more questions.

"You got the name of a doctor?'' Leah asked.

Roman nodded. He didn't want to expand on the conversation. Leah took the piece of paper with the number and he noticed her hand shook slightly.

"I'm not ready,'' she said.

Roman nodded. "Just keep it." This was one thing he couldn't push. Only Leah could decide she was ready to seek medical treatment. He had to let her call the shots, whether he liked it or not.

A knock sounded on the front door of the bar. Roman strode across the floor, pulled back the bolt. Behind him, Leah muted the television.

"I'm Officer Striker, with the Thunder Key PD. Are you Mr. Bradshaw?"

Roman shook the officer's hand. "Thank you for coming by."

Striker was a short man, wiry, possessing a steady, even gaze that conveyed confidence.

"This is Leah...Wells." Dammit, he wanted to say Leah Bradshaw, but for now, until they knew more about who or what was behind the man with the camera and gun stalking Leah, it was best to stick with the identity under which she'd created this life in Thunder Key.

As much as Roman hated it.

Leah came forward, shook the officer's hand.

The three of them settled at a booth. Roman slid in next to Leah, and both of them faced the policeman opposite. Roman laid out the notebook with the names and other notes he'd made from his conversation with Leah the night before.

"You mentioned a possible intrusion into Ms. Wells's apartment," the detective began. "And someone watching her, photographing her."

"I noticed him a couple of days ago in the bar," Leah said, not content to let the officer and Roman discuss her as if she weren't there. "At first, I just thought he was photographing the bar—a lot of tourists do that. Then I realized he was taking pictures of me. But still, I thought it might be nothing.'' She gave a light shrug.

''Then what?'' Striker probed.

''He was talking on a cell phone, then I thought I saw a gun inside his windbreaker. Joey—the cook here—asked him if he was carrying a gun, and he left.''

''Earlier she thought someone had been in her apartment,'' Roman interjected. ''And she's had some odd phone calls.''

''Any threats?''

Leah shook her head. *I know who you are. I know what you've done.* As much as he didn't like it, Roman knew Leah was wise to leave that part out of her statement. It could lead to questions neither of them wanted to answer right now. Not as long as she was living in Thunder Key under an assumed name.

''All right.'' Striker took notes. ''About the apartment, you mentioned nothing was taken.''

''Nothing was taken, as far as I can tell,'' Leah answered. ''I'm not positive anyone was in there, actually. But I *felt* as if someone had been there. Things were moved. Everything was just…off.''

''I'll take prints,'' Striker said. He went on to question her about who else had been in the apartment and to get a description of the man. Roman promised to make a photocopy of his own notes before he left. They contained Leah's list of friends, places she frequented.

''We saw the man again yesterday morning,'' Roman summed up. ''On the beach. He was watching Leah, taking pictures again. And I definitely saw a gun. We know he's been watching her, and possibly he's been in her apartment. What we don't know is why or who he is.''

"I've got a print kit in my cruiser," the officer said. "I'll be right back."

When Striker finished up in Leah's apartment, he shook hands with Roman, then Leah, before leaving. He'd taken Leah's and Roman's prints as well, and would be coming back later to take the staff's prints. "To rule them out," he said.

"This sucks," Leah said when the policeman was gone. "Now my friends are being dragged into my problems."

Joey came in through the rear door.

"I need to explain why Officer Striker will be coming back," Leah said. "To Joey and the other staff."

"Explain what?" Joey asked, approaching the bar.

Leah gave the cook an abbreviated version of the current situation that didn't include the small detail that Roman was her husband.

"I hate this," she finished. "I'm so sorry."

"I don't mind," Joey said, his worried eyes on Leah.

"I mind." She looked more stressed out than ever. "I just want this to end. I want to stop feeling as if I need to be looking over my shoulder, wondering if someone's there, watching me, photographing me." She squeezed her eyes shut for a minute. "This is crazy."

Roman reached out, took her hand. She lifted pain-filled eyes to him. "You need to take a break," he said. "You need to get away from the bar, away from Thunder Key."

"I agree," Joey put in. "Take the day off, Leah. I'll call in some extra help if we get busy." The look the cook gave Roman now was less wary, more grateful. At least Joey was starting to trust Roman.

As for Leah…

"Okay," she said after a long beat.

Maybe, just maybe, she was beginning to trust him after all.

"You've got to be kidding," Leah said when they arrived at their destination, several Keys over on the Overseas Highway.

Roman took her hand in his as they walked past topiary dolphins and mermaids that lined the paved entrance to the marine park. The place teemed with families as the gates opened for the day.

He seemed content to fall into the moment, and that scared her. A complex braid of thoughts and fears tumbled around her head and she had no idea how she could forget them, even for a few hours.

"Are you sure you're a financial stuffed shirt from New York City?" she asked, surprised by Roman's choice in activity for the day. But it hadn't been his first surprise. He'd started off by stopping at a roadside ice-cream stand.

"No day can be all bad that starts with ice cream," he'd said, handing her a cone filled with two heavy scoops of chocolate ripple. She'd taken a lick of the sweet concoction and his eyes had rested on her mouth for a long beat until he'd started the car again.

Little bird wings had fluttered in her chest.

They'd made the drive from Thunder Key with the windows wide open. The air was perfect, the oncom-

ing storm brewing in the Atlantic having brought the
temps down from the usual August heat to something
almost springlike. The only detour had been a Key
deer-spotting expedition onto No Name Key where the
endearingly diminutive animals were easy to spot on
the gulfside shoulder of the road, munching bougain-
villea flowers.

"Do you see a financial stuffed shirt here?" Roman
said now, looking around theatrically as they lined up
at the marine park gate. "I'm a footloose soon-to-be
beach bar owner from the Florida Keys. I don't even
wear a watch." He nodded at his bare wrist. "No cell
phone. No laptop. I have ice cream for breakfast and
nachos for lunch."

"What do you have for dinner?"

Leah's belly turned over at the look in his dark,
dangerous eyes that suggested *she* was on the menu.
Oh, God. She found him so attractive.

He didn't blink an eye as he paid an outrageous sum
for their entry into the park.

"It's crowded," he commented. "When a storm
starts heading in, the tourists don't head out?"

"Not right away. They won't go anywhere unless
they're sure it'll really hit us," Leah said. "Do you
know how much money people spend for a vacation
in the Keys?"

It was hard for her to remember that money was no
object to Roman Bradshaw. If she'd known they'd be
coming to the marine park, she'd have grabbed a local
paper and scanned it for coupons. The tourist papers
and brochures frequently included discounts to the islands' attractions.

He might not be a financial stuffed shirt these days,

but he was obscenely rich nonetheless. She still couldn't imagine how she had fit into his top-flight Manhattan lifestyle.

"Hey." He leaned in and placed a light kiss on her mouth, and his eyes turned sober as he seemed to sense her momentary hesitation. "Let's go have fun. If you get tired, we'll sit down or just go back. Deal?"

"Okay," she agreed, but she realized she felt less tired already. Which probably had something to do with the way Roman's eyes made her feel every time he looked at her. Alive and full of…hope.

But she was so afraid to hope.

He didn't give her any more time to think for the next several hours. The marine park was built on the site of several abandoned quarries, but was now home to a saltwater lagoon containing everything from dolphins to sea lions. After winding their meandering way past shark, turtle and ray tanks, they settled in for the dolphin show. Roman slung his arm casually around Leah's shoulders as they sat near the front, and he laughed when they got sprayed by a dolphin that leaped in the water right in front of them.

At the sea lion exhibition, he dared Leah to join the kids hugging and kissing the friendly creatures, and he snapped photos of her with the throwaway camera he'd picked up in one of the park shops.

"I'll take one of you together," a smiling mother, who'd just finished snapping photos of three giggling girls, offered.

Roman immediately handed the camera over, put his arms around Leah's waist and pulled her saltwater-damp head against his broad chest as the woman took their picture. Leah tried not to think about the fact that this was just more of that fragile facade from this morning.

They weren't really two lovers out for a day of magic in the park. They were two strangers, torn apart by time and fate and something else dark and hidden.

They dried off as they ate a late lunch in a park café where a slideshow of Keys images played endlessly against a side wall. There were photographs mounted under glass on every table.

"So tell me, Roman Bradshaw Version 2.0," Leah said, keeping her voice casual even as she delved into a serious topic. "Why did you come to Thunder Key?"

Roman looked at her for a long moment. He pushed back the plate of food he'd nearly finished. "After I lost you, I tried to go back to work, but it was…empty. It had meant so much to me, building the company my family founded. Or I thought it did. I grew up in the business."

"Do you miss it?"

He shook his head. "I don't miss it at all."

"But why…here? Why Thunder Key?" Returning to the place where they'd honeymooned couldn't have been easy for him. "It just seems as if that would be painful to you."

"It hurt like hell," he said, and Leah felt her heart move into her throat. He was being honest with her, and that couldn't be easy, either, considering the shaky ground their relationship stood on at this point. "But I knew I needed to find a way to heal, to make some kind of peace with myself and move on."

Was that where this was headed? Roman would heal, make peace with what happened, move on as soon as the situation was resolved? *Just let it be what it was—something we both wanted, needed.* That's what he'd said this morning about their lovemaking.

Leah bit her lip, watched him a moment.

"You keep telling me what a bastard you were," she said finally. Was he protecting her, helping her, to relieve his guilt of the past, or did he still care about her, possibly love her? No matter what he said about not being able to believe she'd done anything wrong, it was also clear he was holding back. She just didn't know what to think, or feel, and the worse part was that she could so easily see herself falling for him...again.

"I was attracted to you because you were different, Leah," he said plainly. "Different from everything I'd known all my life. You were open, affectionate, caring. There was nothing cold about you. My family— *cold and rigid* doesn't even begin to describe them."

The more Leah heard about his parents, the more she dreaded the possibility of ever meeting them again.

"They're not bad people," he added quickly. "But they're very conservative, traditional, bound by rules that you didn't seem to even care about. You constantly amazed me. You had priorities that were so foreign to me, and as a result, we had a lot of conflicts."

"What kind of conflicts?" She was curious.

"Mostly the way we spent our time. Or I should say the way I spent my time. Which was mostly working. You always wanted to drag me off somewhere, forget work, and I always resisted."

"You dragged me away from work today," she said.

His eyes shone such a deep blue. They crinkled slightly at the corners, and she realized she saw him smile in his eyes before his mouth joined in a slightly wry expression.

"Tables are turned," he said.

"So why tell me all this?" she asked. "I don't remember it. Why tell me you were such a bastard?"

He held her gaze for several long seconds. "There's no moving on without facing the past, Leah," he said quietly. "For both of us."

She sipped her drink. There was so much to the puzzle of their marriage that she couldn't put together. "So what else did you do in New York? You know, besides work?"

"Run. We had that in common. I wasn't much of one for hobbies. Even running was like work. Till I started running with you."

"Oh?" She waited, interested.

"You drove me nuts. You would stop and smell the flowers. Literally." His hard lips curved a bit again, and heat zinged through her. He had such a killer smile. "You made me do lots of things I didn't want to do."

"Like what? Besides smelling flowers?" The idea of big, bad Roman smelling flowers amused her.

"Museums, kiddie rides, circuses, you name it, you were always getting me to go somewhere and play. If I tried to say no, you'd make up some stupid holiday and say I had to do it."

She remembered the holiday he'd made up to get her to walk on the beach with him.

"And did you? Do it, I mean?" she asked.

A shadow shifted across his eyes. "Sometimes."

She felt the same shadow fall over herself. "I hardly ever go out," she told him. "The bar is my comfort zone, I guess. It's where I feel safe." Until now. Now she didn't feel safe anywhere. Even here, on another Key, in a park crowded with children. She found herself wanting to look around, see if a mysterious man with a camera and a gun was watching her.

"How did your family feel about me?" she asked suddenly. She just had an instinctive feeling about it, from everything he'd said. It was the same feeling she had about cats.

"They didn't approve."

She nodded. "That's what I figured."

His family wasn't likely to approve of her now, either. Roman was a grown man and he'd clearly had the backbone to marry her in spite of their objections, but that didn't make the situation any easier. Now he'd not only married the wrong woman, he was here with her in the Keys. This was some kind of emotional journey he'd made down here to the place where they'd honeymooned, and even he couldn't know how he'd feel when this was all over.

He was smart not to make promises about the future to her, and she would be smart to remember it.

After lunch they stopped in the midway. Roman insisted on spending an inordinate amount of time winning her a stuffed dolphin. "Dolphins mean good luck," he told her when he finally managed to knock down the required number of smiling ducks off the range. He looked boyish as he did it, and as much as she knew she couldn't have had much of a childhood growing up in a series of foster homes, she doubted

Roman had had much of one, either, in the austere Bradshaw dynastic household.

Then he'd met her and she'd made him play. Now it was his turn to make her play. *Tables are turned,* he'd said. He'd told her enough times that he was a bastard, but the truth was he was sweet—in a dangerous, break-your-heart kind of way that was threatening to tear her up inside because none of this was real. It was that facade again. And it could shatter so easily.

They took a spin in the Ferris wheel. High above the park, the chain of islands dotted out to the gray-blue stormy horizon. And Leah felt as if they were alone for that moment, just she and Roman, on top of the world. Above the storm and everything else unknown that lay ahead.

Then the wheel spun them back to earth.

Their last stop was a coin-operated fortune machine labeled Fortune Bob. Roman slipped quarters in the coin drop and Leah's heart stumbled as she pulled out the slip of paper and read it.

"'Fortune Bob says, Accept the next proposition you hear and you won't regret it,'" she read. She looked at Roman. His eyes flared. "Am I in trouble now?" she asked, her heart in her throat. He could probably propose just about anything and she'd do it, fortune reading or not.

"Depends on what you consider trouble," Roman answered.

Clouds were moving in as they left the midway. It was early evening, but a stormy twilight dusted the sky. A band played music under a canopied stage in the middle of the park.

"I think I felt a sprinkle hit my nose," Leah said, turning her face upward.

"Perfect for dancing in the rain."

"We're going to get soaked," she said. "Notice how everyone else is heading for shelter."

"You're not going to risk Fortune Bob's wrath, are you?" Roman pulled her into his arms. He smelled like rain and wishes, and she didn't care how wet they got.

She was extremely aware of him. His body, molded to hers, felt unbelievably wonderful, all big shoulders and strong muscles and security. They barely moved, only swayed as the sultry music resonated around them.

The rain fell harder. "I told you we were going to get wet," she said, lifting her head to look up at him, still in his arms. But she wasn't thinking about the rain. She was thinking about the incredible sex they'd shared last night and wondering how the hell she was going to stop herself from doing it again.

Even now, with his hands on her body, his mouth a breath away, all she could think about was wanting his heat inside her once more. It was as if his taste, his touch, his scent, were threaded into her very soul. And had been for a long time.

"Leah?"

She swallowed thickly. "Yes?"

"Are you all right?"

No, I'm scared to death of falling in love with you. "I'm tired," she told him.

"Let's go home," he said, and she didn't know if he meant the bar or the White Seas, but it struck her that whatever he'd meant, it had been Thunder Key, not New York. Her heart flip-flopped as he reached up, grazed her jaw in a tender caress, then pushed back a tangled, damp tendril of hair off her cheek. Her arms crept up around his neck and he leaned down, capturing her mouth. The proof of his arousal pressed against her.

Then the sky really opened up.

He ended the kiss, looked at her for a hot, hungry beat with something fathomless and lost in his eyes. Rain streamed down his face, and it took her a few seconds to realize they were both sopping wet.

"Run," he said, and she let out a little scream as they raced across the park to the gates. They reached the car and slammed inside. As they drove away, Leah punched the radio buttons on the dash stereo, adding a soft play of music to the tap and splash of the rain outside the car.

She laid her head back on the headrest, realizing she really was tired.

"Leah." She felt someone touching her shoulder, and blinked. "You fell asleep. I hate to wake you up, but we need to get inside."

She looked around, realized they were in front of the main hotel building of the White Seas.

"I need to check in with the Shark and Fin," she said automatically. She couldn't remember the last time she'd taken an entire day off work. "Make sure everything went okay today."

Hotel attendants appeared as if by magic to whisk the car away. Roman and Leah walked inside, protected from the rain by the covered lobby portico. He led her through the marbled entrance area, then out to the bungalow path. They raced down the twisty, Spanish lime-scented stones to the little cigar maker's cottage that was Roman's.

·They stumbled into the bungalow. Rain-kissed air blew across the darkened room, tangling the terrace sheers.

A shadow lunged for the open garden door.

Chapter 12

"Get hotel security. Press eight on the phone," Roman said as he pushed past Leah.

"No!" she cried, the word torn from her raggedly as she tried to stop him. In that fraction of a second when he met her panicked eyes, all the doubts about their relationship ceased to matter. She was scared—for him. The rush of emotion was so intense it nearly bowled him over. But he didn't have time to feel. He had to act, now. The figure had already disappeared.

He left Leah behind, gave chase through the garden doors, wishing with all his heart he was armed with more than an absolute will to stop this thing, whatever it was, that was happening to Leah.

Crashing into the rain-soaked night, Roman spotted the man rounding the corner of the next bungalow, heading for the beach—and the hammock of thick trees. Breath seared Roman's lungs, but no way was he slowing down. He charged forward, praying hotel security wouldn't be too far behind. If the man reached the hammock of trees, he'd lose himself in the night-thick tropical morass. Sand flew up as he raced onto the beach.

Thank God he was a runner. The other man was already winded, but nothing was stopping Roman. The intruder charged into the dark trees nonetheless. Roman left the wet beach, threw himself into the jungle-thick hammock, tackling the man just as he stumbled over a root. Something stung Roman's cheek, a branch or thorny vine. They hit the ground with a jarring thud that nearly knocked the wind out of Roman. Something tumbled forward out of the man's hand, knocked back off a tree trunk. A gun.

Blood surged through Roman's veins. Whatever he was going to do, he had to do it fast. He hadn't trained for tackling criminals on Wall Street, but he knew right then and there he'd do anything for Leah. When the man tried to scramble away, Roman yanked him back down by the collar of his jacket and slammed a fist into the side of his face. The man was stunned just long enough for Roman to lunge for the gun.

With no hesitation whatsoever he pressed the barrel under the man's chin. In the twilight he recognized the man from the beach. The man who'd been watching Leah. And now he'd been in their bungalow. Why?

"If I were you, I wouldn't move," Roman told him.

The man swore. The sound of voices rang out from a distance. Hotel security. Rain dripped down through the trees. The man's eyes flared in the dimness.

"Who the hell are you?" Roman demanded, his blood jerking through his veins.

"I don't have to tell you anything." The man seemed to regain his senses from the daze of Roman's blow. But he didn't move other than to gasp for breath. The cold push of the gun's barrel beneath his chin held him immobilized.

"You can tell me or you can tell the police. Hotel security is on the way."

The man swore again. "I'm a private detective." His voice shook slightly. "I have a license. If you'll let me get my wallet—"

Not a chance. "Where is it?"

"Inside my jacket. There's a pocket—"

Roman kept the barrel trained beneath the man's chin, used his other hand to rip open the man's jacket. He found the wallet, flipped it open. The P.I. license was in the front plastic sleeve. He jerked it sideways, dumping the card out, and tilted it in his hand till he could barely make out the name in the stormy twilight through the trees. Norman Robertson. State of Florida. His father had lied to him once about hiring a private eye to investigate Leah. And now it appeared he'd lied to him again yesterday on the phone. Roman's heart beat with a sick, thudding rhythm. Anger flooded him.

"I have a permit for this gun," Robertson said.

"You don't have a permit for breaking and entering," Roman grated, throwing the wallet down. He tucked the P.I. license in his back pocket. "You don't have a permit to stalk my wife." Roman bit out each word. "Who hired you? Or do you want to wait and explain it from a jail cell?"

"You don't want me to explain anything to the police, Bradshaw," the man hissed. "Your *wife*—" he spat the word "—is living here under a false identity.

I'm not stalking her. I wasn't going to do anything to hurt her. I was just looking for information.''

Roman's heart tripped, turned to ice. ''What do you know about my wife?''

''More than you do.''

Roman tossed aside the gun and grabbed him by the throat. ''Then spill it. Now.''

''Ask your family if you want to know. I work for them, not you. And if you don't want the whole island to know what your family already knows about that wife of yours, you'd better let me go before hotel security gets here.'' The man's glazed eyes locked with Roman's. ''Nobody's trying to hurt your wife, Bradshaw. *She's* the criminal.''

Roman felt like someone had reached in and clamped a fist around his heart. *Nobody's trying to hurt your wife. She's the criminal.* It wasn't possible. No way in hell. He couldn't believe Leah had done anything wrong.

The voices beyond the hammock came closer.

If you don't want the whole island to know…

''My family hired you?'' Roman demanded. ''I guarantee you, you are off the case. Get out of Thunder Key. If I see you near Leah again, I'm not going to be responsible for what happens to you. Do you understand?''

''Fine, whatever. They didn't tell me you were insane.''

Roman jerked off him, picked up the gun and emptied the bullets from the chamber before tossing it back. ''Get out of here.''

He had to find out what his parents knew about

Leah. And he had to protect her. Even if that meant letting this creep get away.

The man staggered to his feet. He scrambled for his emptied gun and his wallet in the underbrush. "Where's my license?"

"In my pocket. Be happy you're not losing it permanently for breaking and entering." Roman raised his voice. "Now get lost!"

The man hesitated for about two seconds, then disappeared into the mesh of trees. Roman stepped out of the woods, nearly barreling into two uniformed hotel security guards. He felt out of breath and his whole body strummed with an awful tension. He'd been around the hotel long enough for them to recognize him.

"We had a call on an intruder, sir," one of the guards said, out of breath himself.

"Someone was in my bungalow when I entered it," Roman said. "I chased him, but lost him in the trees."

The guard spoke into a walkie-talkie, then nodded at the other guard. "See if you can find him."

The other guard took off.

"He's long gone," Roman said. "I'm not sure if anything was taken, so we should go back and check. But I think we interrupted him before he got a chance." Let them think it was a burglary attempt. He didn't care. He just didn't want anyone asking questions about Leah.

"Sir, we take pride in our security here. We should have security tapes that can show us who was on the property tonight, and might help us nail him. Was the bungalow locked?"

"Yes." He had to get to Leah. He didn't care about

any of this. "I need to get back to my—" Wife. He wanted to say wife, but he bit back the word.

If you want the whole island to know... For now, till he found out what was really in Leah's past, it was for the best to keep her identity under wraps. He couldn't believe it, but obviously the detective had found out something in Leah's former life. Before she met Roman. Before they married. And his parents knew it. He had to get the information.

Then he'd deal with it, whatever it was.

What if she was on the run? Thoughts rioted in his head. What if she had been on the run when he met her? What if she was wanted for a crime? Would he take her away from here, now that she'd been found?

His chest wound tight at the thought, but he knew without a doubt he would do anything it took to protect her. But what if he couldn't protect her? What if it was something so terrible...

He couldn't let himself think that way.

"I have to get back to my bungalow. I have a...friend."

"A member of the hotel staff is with her, sir," the guard said. "The police are on the way. We'll need both of you to make a statement when they get here."

Roman nodded. "Fine."

The guard spoke into his walkie-talkie again. The other guard scrambled back through the trees, onto the beach. "No sign of him."

Thank God. Roman charged back across the beach. The bungalow. Leah. He needed to hold her, right now, in his arms, the same way he needed his next breath.

All the lights were on in the bungalow. Leah stood framed in the garden doors.

She ran out to him. He pulled her into his arms.

"I was so worried," she breathed shakily against his chest.

Roman pulled her into the bungalow, into the light. She looked shell-shocked, but she was smiling shakily in relief. God, he didn't want to say anything that would take that smile off her face. He saw a female hotel employee waiting by the door.

"I was so scared," Leah whispered. "Don't ever do that again! You could have been killed. If something had happened to you—"

"Shh. Nothing happened. I'm fine." He wasn't fine, and neither was she, but he had no idea how to tell her. He didn't *want* to tell her.

The phone in the bungalow rang sharply. Leah almost jumped out of her skin.

Roman grabbed the phone.

"Mr. Bradshaw? An officer is here from the Thunder Key PD. He's on his way to your bungalow now."

Roman thanked the clerk and hung up. "We're going to have to make a statement," he explained to Leah. "It shouldn't take long."

Especially since he'd be lying through his teeth to the officer.

"Your cheek," Leah said suddenly, and reached up to touch him. "You have a cut."

Roman hadn't even felt it. "Must have happened when I chased the guy into the trees," he said.

Leah's eyes darkened for a second, the fear returning. Fear for him.

"I'm fine," he told her again. She had no reason to

fear for him, at least that much was true. It was Leah who could be in trouble. But at least she was safe. No one on Thunder Key was out to hurt her. There was no stalker. But there was no lessening in the tension in Roman's body. Something terrible was in her past and he couldn't rest till he knew what it was.

There was a knock on the door. The hotel employee opened it. An officer in a Thunder Key Police uniform entered the bungalow. The hotel employee closed it as she left.

The officer shook Leah's and Roman's hands, and they sat at the table and chair near the garden doors. Roman briefly explained the report they'd made earlier in the day about the strange phone calls and the man following Leah. He left out everything else. The officer took prints from both the garden doors and the bungalow entrance.

Finally satisfied, the officer finished. "I'll be collecting the security tapes from the hotel," he said. "I'll let you know if anything turns up. If you look around later and realize something was stolen after all, give me a call at the station."

"Thank you." Roman escorted him to the door. He turned back to Leah. She stood by the bed, exhausted and pale.

"Let me see to that cut," she said softly, reaching for him.

"It's nothing," he said. "Forget it." A bleakness hit him, nearly doubled him over. He had no idea what was ahead for her. She looked so innocent, so beautiful and fragile.

She stared up at him, her eyes hurting, worried. "Something's wrong."

His heart twisted.

"What aren't you telling me?" Her voice sounded hollow in the now-empty bungalow.

He sat her down on the bed, tugged her into his arms, touched her hair, her back, felt the softness of her arms.

"Roman!"

He drew back enough to see her face. "The man's name is Norman Robertson. He's a private detective, hired by my family. I didn't tell the police I caught up with him because…I didn't want there to be questions. About you." He pulled out the investigator's license and showed it to her.

"Oh, God," she breathed. She looked scared again.

"The important thing to know is that the man who was watching you, photographing you, isn't going to hurt you. You're not in danger from him." She could be in danger, but it was another sort of danger. Danger from the law, not from some crazed stalker. He didn't want to tell her that. She was terrified enough. She'd been through enough.

When he found out the truth, it would be soon enough to tell her. Right now he didn't know anything, and what he had to say would only upset her more.

He hated not telling her everything. She deserved the truth—both of them did. But what if she ran? What if she'd been running that night her car went over the bridge?

There was no way he was risking it. He had to find out for himself, and then he could prove to her that nothing would tear them apart.

And he prayed that was true.

''You don't have to worry about him anymore. He's off the case.''

''Are you sure?''

''I'll make sure.'' He wanted to call his parents right that minute, but his father had lied to him on the phone just yesterday. There was no way he'd know if he was getting the truth now.

He had to talk to his parents face-to-face. He didn't know whether Mark had told them about Leah, or if they'd sent the detective down here on their own just to check up on him. It didn't matter. All that mattered was that it stop.

And that when it was over, he still had Leah.

''I'm going to have to go to New York,'' he told her. ''Tomorrow. I'll come back tomorrow night if I can, or the next morning at the latest.''

''Why?'' She looked as if she wanted to cling to him, but she kept her arms at her sides.

''I need to speak to my family,'' he said. ''It's time for them to understand that they have no role to play in what's happening here between us. And maybe I can get some answers for you. I have to find out what the investigator told them about you. He wouldn't tell me anything. But my family will. I'm not going to give them a choice.'' He struggled to temper the anger in his voice. This wasn't the time. He would deal with his parents when he got to New York. Right now Leah needed him.

''I can't go with you. I'm not ready.'' Her voice shook.

''I know.'' He didn't want to leave her tomorrow, but he had no choice. He had to find out the truth. ''I won't be gone more than one night,'' he swore to her.

The silence seemed to ache between them. There were still so many unknowns. Their future was like a dark lake and he couldn't see the bottom.

· Tension was visible in Leah's shoulders, and Roman pulled her back into his arms. He prayed he wouldn't find out something in New York that would hurt her. His heart was beating an unmistakable message. After eighteen months, the feelings he had for her were stronger than ever, but he couldn't bear to put them into words, even in his own mind. Not when their future was still lost in the fog of Leah's memories. He couldn't stand to lose her again. He would do whatever he had to do to make sure he didn't. But ultimately, he was afraid it was out of his control. Maybe even out of Leah's.

He didn't want her to lose hope, though.

"You don't have to be scared anymore, Leah. Whatever is in your past, we'll deal with it together."

"Don't make any promises," she said softly.

Her words tore him apart. He could feel her heart pounding. He didn't know what to say to her, but he couldn't have stopped himself from lying down on the bed and pulling her into his arms if he'd tried. Her clothes were still damp, but she was warm and willing and exactly what he needed. He was careful, tenderly aware of her still-bandaged hand. She was ready, willing to give herself to him, wanting him so much it made his chest hurt and his eyes sting.

"I missed you so much," he whispered against her mouth. He wanted this night, in this once-honeymoon bed, to never end. He wanted anything to be possible. He pulled her against him and kissed her tenderly, soulfully, and he pretended all those things were true.

Leah's head swam and blood coursed warm and heavy through her veins. He slipped his hands beneath her blouse and the sensation of his fingers against her skin was beyond description. Everything about the way he held her, kissed her, was right, like a homecoming. And she didn't want to think about anything except the way his hands, his mouth, felt on her willing body.

He tugged up on her blouse and she lay back on the soft bed beside him as he pulled it over her head. With one swift move, he yanked his own shirt aside, then reached for the nearly-transparent cream bra she wore. He traced the lace edging for a moment, his gaze holding hers, questioning, asking permission. She reached for the front clasp, and the filmy covering came apart.

As if he couldn't resist another second, he cupped the soft heat of her breasts, buried his face in her, kissed her, inhaled her, until she was frantically searching for the buckle of his belt, the button on his jeans.

She wanted him so very badly. The zipper stuck and she fumbled with it, her fingers shaking with the need that burned inside her like a ferocious fire.

"I need you now," she whispered as he swept his tongue again across her sensitive nipple.

He pulled up his head and she was lost for a wild beat in his hungering eyes. "Where?" he asked huskily. "Tell me where."

"Here." She pushed at her pants, almost frantic. She wanted these clothes standing between them to be gone. He leaned back, tore them off her hips, down and away. She worried again at his zipper and this time he helped her, until they were both naked in the shrouded bed.

Leah touched his smooth, muscled chest, closing her eyes now, experiencing the pure heaven of his skin beneath her fingertips. He was so warm, so solid, so safe to her in this world that hadn't been safe in a very long time. Her universe narrowed to only him, only now, only here.

And then he was kissing her, touching her, sweeping his hands all over her body, and she was in ecstasy. It was sweet and simple and natural. She reached between them, encircling his arousal, and she felt his own passion kick into overdrive. He explored her body, as well, and she responded instantly to his touch. She drew in a quivery intake of air. Sweetly slick with need, she was ready for him. Lifting her hips into his hand, she encouraged him, but he wouldn't be rushed.

"We have all night," he breathed against her lips, then trailed lower, farther, until his tongue entered that sweetest core. He coaxed and tormented the swollen, aching heat of her until she burned white-hot.

"Please, Roman, now." And then her voice no longer worked. If this was torment, it was the most wonderful she'd ever known. A whirlwind of emotions and heightened sensations flooded her. He stripped her bare of any inhibition, leaving her ruled by only passion and his amazing touch. It was primitive and real, like nothing else had been for eighteen months.

His hands were everywhere, his mouth everywhere.

"Yes, yes." And it was all she could do to moan that one word over and over as his tongue dipped within her again. Then she splintered from the inside out.

She arched, then fell back on the bed, shattered and dizzied. Slowly, so slowly, he raised himself over her. Almost unable to lift her bone-melted hand, she reached for his hardness, and his instinct reflexive response shot a thrill through her, and the heat that had spun her apart a moment before rose again to fever pitch.

With impossible deliberation, he lowered himself onto her. She gripped his buttocks, guiding him as he entered her. The muscles in his powerful arms tautened and his eyes glistened as they held on to hers. Still, he was barely inside her, the intimate tip of him parting her.

A fraction at a time, he slid deeper, staring into her eyes all the while. And he covered his mouth with hers, swallowing her moan of pleasure as he sheathed himself fully inside her. Leah moved with him as he set an excruciatingly languorous pace accompanied by more of his penetrating, heart-searing kisses.

Then he increased the pace and she tore her mouth away to fling her head back, eyes closed, her hair flying wildly around her. The sound she heard herself make was almost inhuman, then she was deafened by the passionate rush of her blood as sweet arrows shot through her, exploding in little stars of fire. She became aware then of his release and she opened her eyes. He went over that tender-furious edge with his gaze on her, her name on his lips before he sank down over her.

She could feel his heart thundering in time with her own, feel his breaths against her cheek, his arms tightly wound around her. Then he lowered beside her, pulling her snug in the crook of his strong shoulder, no sound but their pulse beats and the tap of rain on the bungalow roof and the plaintive slap of palm fronds in the wind outside.

She slept without a single dream.

Morning came in a fearful rush. Leah opened her eyes, saw Roman beside her, heard the rain still splashing down on the terrace and blinked back a sudden sting of tears.

He would go to New York today. He would find out the truth, whatever it was.

And they might never share a night like that again.

But Leah knew that even if they didn't, she had not one regret for the past two nights in his arms. Making love with Roman had been the most powerful experience of her life. He made her feel cherished. He swept her away with his sourcerous mouth and hands. And she knew it wasn't just Thunder Key that was her home. It was Roman. *He* was her home, her haven, her sweetest dream.

Today it might all be over if her greatest dread about her past turned out to be true. But she would always have these two nights with Roman.

Sleeping, he looked so at peace she hated to wake him. His dark hair was tousled, his chin rough with a night's beard growth. He was dangerously sexy without doing a thing. Her heart flipped as she remembered how he'd held her gaze while he'd exploded with passion. As she watched him, he opened his eyes and met hers again.

There was heat in his ocean-storm depths.

But he was leaving, and she suddenly couldn't bear it.

"I'll drive you to the airport in Key West," she said, and started to turn away, determined to get into the shower before she could cry.

"Not yet." He pulled her back, and she saw the emotion lurking in his amazing depths. "We still have time."

"Not much time."

"Enough."

His tortured gaze seared her and she closed her eyes, unable to endure the pain of knowing, seeing, how much he felt for her. Their relationship stood on such uncertain ground, and they both knew it.

What if she was wanted for some crime she couldn't remember? Would he come back—to turn her in or to take her on the run? Could she let him run away with her? She had run away once already. Why? She had gone alone then. Even if she wasn't on the run, wasn't wanted by the law, he might be repulsed by what he would learn about her today.

And despite his words to the contrary, her actions of the past could change his feelings for her entirely.

Thinking hurt so much, and when she felt his mouth brush her lips, she choked back a sob as she tangled her arms around his neck and pulled him close. There was nothing slow about their lovemaking now, not when he was on the verge of leaving her. It was reckless and fast and so intense, it was like hurtling away on a shooting star—blinding.

When it was over, he held on to her as if he'd never let go.

Later, the drive to Key West was quiet. When they arrived at the small airport, Roman didn't get out right away.

"There's something I need to tell you," he said. "I should have told you before. You have a right to know."

Leah waited, her throat filling with something ominous.

His eyes bored into hers, somehow hollow. "When they found your car, there were divorce papers inside a briefcase. You were planning to leave me."

She felt sick. "Why?"

He shook his head. "That's a question only you can answer, Leah."

The Shark and Fin was nearly empty. The storm kept even the regulars at bay as the TV over the bar blared out a flash-flood warning. The tropical storm—now an official hurricane—was still traveling an unpredictable path, and whether or not it would miss the Keys remained in question. But as it picked up speed and pummeled toward the coast, it was drenching everything for hundreds of miles in all directions.

Stress made Leah's shoulders tight, but it wasn't the storm she feared. It was the thought of Roman, right now, flying toward Miami where he'd pick up a connection to New York. She'd stood on the rain-soaked airport tarmac, watched the small plane take off in the soggy sky, waving at the tiny piece of his face she could pick out in the plane window. He'd disappeared into the stormy clouds. Even if he wanted to, she wasn't sure he'd be able to make good on his promise to be back that night or even the next morning. Weather could easily shut the Key West airport down by then if the flash-flood warnings held true.

He'd made her promise that if things changed, if the

hurricane threatened Thunder Key, she would head for the mainland. Before leaving the White Seas, he'd made reservations at the Grand Palm Hotel in Miami for the next two nights.

"Just in case you have to evacuate," he'd told her. "The room is in both our names. I'll meet you there."

He had thought of everything, but she knew he couldn't plan for what he'd find out in New York about her past. And as for the divorce, she was still in shock. She could see now why he'd held back. He was afraid that when she remembered everything, she would leave him. And all she longed to do was tell him there was no way that would happen, but neither of them knew what he would find out in New York.

The hours passed in anxious beats. She sent Shanna home halfway through the day, leaving just herself and Joey to run the bar. By early evening she sent Joey home. He helped her board up the windows before he left.

"You never know what'll happen during the night," he said. "The hurricane is turning southward. Keep your radio on. You have batteries, right?"

"I'll be fine," she told him. She turned the bar's sign to Closed and locked up. Morrie's pickup was gassed up. If she had to evacuate before morning, she was ready. Carrying her battery-powered radio, she headed up the stairs to the apartment where she hadn't slept in two nights.

Wind whistled outside and rain slapped down on the rooftop. She was halfway up the stairs before she stopped, realized the pounding she heard wasn't part of the storm.

Someone was knocking on the door of the bar.

Chapter 13

It was the longest day of Roman's life. He barely made his connection in Miami. Making last-minute flight arrangements, he'd been routed through Atlanta and landed with a thirty-minute layover. Just enough time to find a phone. He wouldn't have a second to spare once he hit New York, especially if he wanted to get back to Florida tonight. And even one night away from Leah was too much.

While he had no intention of getting into the discussion about Robertson on the phone, he needed to make sure his parents knew he was coming. Of course, if Robertson had been in contact with them, they wouldn't be surprised by his arrival.

"Mr. Bradshaw isn't in today," came the clipped voice of Rita, his father's secretary.

Walter Bradshaw never took a day off.

"Is he sick?" And Roman knew it would have to

be *really* sick, like having-a-heart-attack sick. Despite the anger simmering in his blood over the private investigator, the idea of something being terribly wrong with his father gave him an immediate stone-sinking sensation in his gut.

"I don't know, sir."

"Is Gen there?" he asked

"She's not in today, either," Rita told him.

Roman called the house. Barbara Bradshaw picked up.

"Roman!" Her cultured voice cracked oddly. "Where are you?"

"I'm at Hartsfield in Atlanta. I'm on my way to New York."

"Thank God."

"Is Dad all right?"

"Dad? Yes, of course, he's fine. I'm so glad you're coming home. We need you here. It's Roman," he heard her telling someone. People streamed around him where he stood in the airport terminal. He missed his mother's next words.

"What?"

"Did Gen call you?"

"No. Why would Gen call me?" He felt his blood pressure going up. He wondered if his parents had roped Gen into mediating with him over the Robertson fiasco. That wouldn't surprise him. He couldn't stop thinking about Leah, back in Thunder Key, and the lonely figure she'd made on the tarmac as his plane had rolled away.

His mother said something but he missed it as the announcement blared that his plane was boarding passengers.

"My flight's boarding," he said. "I'll be there in a couple of hours. I need to talk to you and Dad. I need both of you to be there. I won't have much time. I'm flying back to Thunder Key tonight."

He hung up and raced for the gate.

The Bradshaws' sleek high-rise towered between Madison and Park in a tony Upper East Side neighborhood with double-wide tree-lined streets and money-scented air. The prewar building's marble lobby was as cold as the sprawling apartments housed inside it. Roman had grown up in the four-bedroom penthouse, with its fabulous views of the bustling city stretching in every direction.

He missed Thunder Key, the laidback sense of sea and sun. And Leah.

His mother opened the apartment door. As ever, she appeared the tastefully coiffed Manhattan woman, agelessly elegant. Even at home, she wore a tailored designer suit and was perfectly made up. She was always prepared for company or shopping.

"Roman, you look like you've been in a fight," Barbara said, offering a brittle hug before stepping back to reach her manicured hand for his cheek.

He *was* in a fight—a fight for his future with Leah. But he knew that wasn't what his mother was referring to.

"It's nothing," he said, moving past her through the terrazzo-tiled foyer. "We need to talk."

"Roman."

Her voice stopped him. There was emotion, thick, in his name, and it surprised him. His mother rarely showed emotion. He'd never seen his parents argue.

He'd had big, juicy, incredible arguments with Leah—
and every one of them had ended in even more incredible sex. It was a big part of what had scared him
about her, all that unshuttered emotion—it had just
taken him a long time to realize it. Here, in his parents'
austere home again, it hit him harder than ever.

Why hadn't he told her that he loved her before he
left Thunder Key? But he knew the answer. He had
been afraid. He had lost Leah once, and after he found
her, he had shielded himself from the possible pain of
losing her again. He had kept his emotions in check.
He was as much a fool as he had ever been. Life was
too precarious to let fear rule.

But he couldn't think of that now. The look on his
mother's face threw him—it was almost panicky. And
he realized she was pale beneath that perfect makeup.

"Gen needs you," she said. "I'm glad you're
back."

Barbara put shaking fingers to her mouth, didn't
speak. Roman closed the distance between them, put
his hands on her frail-feeling arms. "What's going
on?"

"Thank God you've come to your senses and come
back to New York, son."

Roman pivoted. Walter Bradshaw, in his customary
dark suit and power tie, filled the opening between the
living room and foyer.

"I'm leaving soon," Roman said succinctly. "I
only came here to tell you to get the hell out of my
life. You and your private investigator."

"What private investigator?" Barbara asked.

Roman spun on her. "The one you hired to follow
Leah around, find out about her past." He turned back

to his father. "You told me you didn't find out anything about Leah's past, but you also told me you
never had her investigated. Now I want the truth. I
want to know what you found out about Leah."

"It's history, son," Walter said. "There's no
point."

"I need to know." Roman steeled himself.

His father shook his head. "You wouldn't listen,"
he said insistently. "We told you there was something
not right about her. She came to the city like she had
no past. Everyone has a past, son. She would have
ruined you."

"What did you find out about Leah?"

"She was involved in a murder when she was seventeen years old," Barbara broke in. "The circumstances were sketchy so she was never officially
charged, but she spent time in a juvenile facility afterward."

"For all we knew," his father added after a tense
moment, "you were married to a murderer."

Roman felt as if he'd been kicked in the gut. His
mind reeled with the tangled memories of all the
things Leah had told him about her past. Her mixed-
up nightmares.

"You honestly think Leah could kill someone?"
The look on his parents' faces was all the answer he
needed. "Did she know you knew about it?" Was that
why she'd left him that night eighteen months ago?
Was she trying to save him from her past? Had his
parents convinced her that she was going to ruin his
life, his political future that he'd never even wanted?
So many questions tore at his mind.

What about the man in the white lab coat she'd

dreamed of running away from? How did that fit in? Was he connected to the juvenile facility? He felt as if he had too many puzzle pieces and they weren't making a complete picture. A part of him wanted to sag in relief that the terrible thing in her past was at least over—she wasn't still wanted for a crime. But something nipped at his gut. The puzzle pieces weren't right.

"It doesn't matter," Walter said. "She's dead—"

"You know damn well she's not dead," Roman cut in, his voice low and his temper spiking. He wanted them to stop lying. About all of it. "I'm sure Robertson has already told you that she's alive, if Mark hasn't."

"What?" Barbara looked like she was about to faint. "That girl is alive?"

Roman stared his mother down. "*That girl* is my wife." He turned back to Walter. "You sent Robertson down there—"

"Who?" Walter asked.

"Norman Robertson. Florida licensed private detective, out of Miami," Roman bit out. He pulled the P.I. license out of his pocket and shoved it into Walter's hand. "Don't lie to me anymore. You had her investigated when we got married, and you lied about it. You admitted that much the other day on the phone. Then you had me followed down to Thunder Key. I want the truth now."

Walter's face turned red. "I didn't have you followed to Thunder Key!"

"Leah's alive?" Barbara repeated.

"She lost her memory after the crash, and she went to the one place she knew—where we spent our honeymoon.'' Roman looked at his father again. ''There's a lot to work out, but I hope—'' his chest tightened ''—I hope we can have a future again.''

The words tore out of his mouth, his heart. He ached inside, and all he wanted was to be finished with this confrontation and get back to Leah. He wanted to say those words to her, not his parents.

He took a steadying breath. ''I don't care what you claim she's done in the past. It doesn't matter to me. If she'll have me, I want to rebuild what we had, our marriage. And if you want to have any relationship with me at all in the future,'' he said succinctly, ''you'll stay out of it.''

''I have no idea who the hell this Robertson is, but I didn't send anyone to Thunder Key,'' Walter said, his hand holding the P.I. license shaking. ''I had Leah investigated after you married her, that's true and I've admitted that. But it wasn't this Norman Robertson character. I've never heard of him. I swear on everything I hold dear that I didn't hire anyone to follow you to Thunder Key. I didn't know she was alive.''

His father's denial hung thick in the foyer. Roman looked at his mother, took in again the shocked blankness in her eyes, and a sense of dread rocked him. He faced his father again, saw the cold snap of truth in Walter's eyes.

''Oh, my God,'' Roman said, suddenly hoarse. His mind spun. ''If you didn't send Robertson down to Thunder Key—''

''I swear to you, son, it wasn't me or your mother.''

''Then who did?'' The man had said he was hired by family. The only other family who knew about Leah was...Mark. But why would Mark take it upon himself to send a private investigator? Nothing was making sense.

"I don't know," Walter said.

"I have to call Leah." Roman charged into the living room, stopped short at the sight that met his eyes. Gen sat huddled on the Italian cognac-colored leather couch, her face buried in her hands, hidden by a curtain of her caramel hair.

She lifted her head. Her eyes were red, her cheeks damp, splotchy. "Roman." His name trembled from her mouth. "He only wanted to help people. That's what he always said about why he became a doctor. He cared, maybe too much, that's all. He helped people other doctors wouldn't help."

"What are you talking about?" All Roman wanted to do was grab the phone, call Leah, but Gen's words hit him across the chest. Dammit, what the hell was wrong with everyone? "Where's Mark? I need to talk to him."

"I thought you knew," Walter said, coming in behind Roman. "I thought that's why you came back."

"Knew what?" Roman was about to lose it. "Is someone going to tell me what the hell is going on here?"

"They shut down Mark's practice," Gen said, panic lacing her voice. "They're saying he illegally distributed pain medication."

"What?" Roman's head reeled. Gen's husband ran one of the most prestigious physical medicine and rehabilitation practices in the city. His patients included celebrities and politicians. Gen had accomplished what Roman hadn't—the perfect marriage by Bradshaw standards. "Who's saying this?"

"The U.S. Attorney's Office," Walter said.

Roman turned, saw his mother crying silently. Now it all made sense—the underlying shock and horror in the apartment.

"It was all over the news this morning," Barbara said shakily. "Didn't you see it?"

He'd been watching the cable weather station, focused on the hurricane approaching the Keys. "No." He sat by Gen, still trying to take it in. His sister buried her face in his chest.

"They charged him with conspiracy to commit health care fraud and taking kickbacks for patient referrals," Gen sobbed against him. "They're saying he overprescribed, created patient dependencies for kickbacks from drug companies and that some of his patients died because of it. They arrested almost everyone in his office, even his office manager and his nurse."

"Where's Mark?" Now he was as shocked as they were. Gen had been married to Mark for ten years. Mark had been the perfect brother-in-law. Roman had been able to count on Mark for anything. And now they were saying he'd killed people? How could this be true?

Gen raised her face to him. "The people on the news were saying he could get life in prison if he's convicted. Millions in fines. They're saying he'll have to forfeit everything—the practice, our house, our bank accounts. They've been investigating him for over eighteen months and I didn't even know it."

The nipping dread in his gut increased. Roman gripped Gen's shoulders. "Where's Mark?" he repeated.

"I don't know!" she cried. "He's gone. He left the house yesterday and I haven't seen him since. He called last night, told me he was working late, but when I woke up this morning, he hadn't been home. I've been calling his cell phone all day, but he doesn't pick up. When the federal authorities raided the office today, Mark wasn't there."

Roman felt his stomach slide. "Did Leah know about any of this?"

"What?" Gen looked blank.

"Why did they start investigating Mark?"

"Somebody went to the police about one of the patients who died," Gen sobbed.

There was a newspaper on the coffee table. For the first time, Roman realized the headline was about Mark. He hunched forward, grabbed it.

Manhattan Pain Specialist Charged in Federal Court, the headline blazed in huge letters. Roman scanned the article, his blood pounding as he read the litany of charges against Dr. Mark Davison that included the deaths of ten patients. He tore open the paper, hunting down the details at the bottom of the article.

The probe had begun with an investigation into the death of a Chelsea woman, Nicole Bates.

Nikki. Leah's roommate and maid of honor.

Fear clamped down on Roman's heart.

"Where the hell is Mark?" he demanded, praying his instincts were wrong.

"Roman!" Barbara cried as he tossed down the paper and charged at the phone on the ornate desk against one wall. He punched in the Shark and Fin's number. A recording came on telling him the connec-

tion was out of service. The storm. Dammit. Roman
threw open the armoire that hid his parents' large television. He clicked immediately to the cable weather
station.

"The hurricane is still threatening the lower Eastern
Seaboard. Evacuations have not yet been ordered, but
are expected by this evening for communities from the
Keys to as far north as Jacksonville if the storm re-
mains on its present course—"

He switched the television off, grabbed the phone
again. "I need information for Miami. Norman Robertson." The operator clicked him through to a recording and the machine automatically dialed the
number.

"What's going on, son?"

Roman ignored his father's question.

A voice picked up on the line. "Robertson."

"Roman Bradshaw. If you've seen the national
news, you know that my brother-in-law has just been
indicted with a federal crime," Roman bit out. "So if
you've been working for him, you're about to have
more trouble than you know what to do with. I want
to know if Mark Davison's the one who hired you to
follow me to Thunder Key. And I want to know if you
have any idea where the hell he is right now."

There was a taut second of cold silence. Then Robertson spoke and Roman's world crashed.

"He was in Miami this morning, that's all I know,"
Robertson said. "I called him last night and he set up
a meeting with me at the Royal Cypress Inn and
Suites. I didn't know about the federal charges, I
swear," he went on, but Roman was already hanging up.

Mark was in Miami? Oh, God…

He turned around to face his sister's stricken face. "I know you don't want to believe Mark could have done anything wrong. I don't want to believe it either." He went to Gen, took her into a brief, fierce hug, struggling with his own disappointment—and nagging fear that somehow this was connected to Leah's disappearance over a year ago. "But if what they're charging him with is true, he could be blaming Leah. She asked a lot of questions after Nikki Bates died. Maybe too many questions."

"That girl was always trouble," Barbara started, but Roman cut her off.

"If she went to the authorities about Nikki's death, she did it to save other lives." He looked around at all of them now. "Nikki Bates was her closest friend. Leah was devastated when she died. And if Leah suspected it wasn't a suicide, that she'd been overprescribed or something—" Everything Leah had told him about her nightmares pummeled at his brain along with those final days and her distress over Nikki's prescriptions.

Had Leah gone to the authorities with her questions? And had Mark somehow known about it? Had Mark forced her car over that bridge? The same Mark who had stood by him during the darkest hours following Leah's disappearance? The crushing betrayal was more than he could process.

"He knew Leah was alive," Roman went on. It was his own fault. *He'd* told Mark about Leah. Guilt nearly killed him. "He's the one who hired Robertson. Mark's in Florida right now and he could be there to hurt Leah. I don't want to believe— Someone made some phone calls, too, and it had to have been Mark. He's the only one who knew she was alive…. Did Mark know about Leah's past?''

Gen's mouth dropped. ''Leah's alive?''

''Yes,'' Walter said heavily. ''Mark knew. I asked Mark to be the one to talk to her, tell her we knew what she'd done, that she was going to ruin your life. Son—'' He broke off as if he didn't know what to say next. He looked sick and old suddenly.

Roman couldn't deal with the anger now, the feelings of betrayal. He was too scared. And he had no time.

He picked up the phone again. ''I need the number for the Royal Cypress Inn and Suites in Miami.'' The operator connected him to a recording and the call was automatically dialed. The hotel picked up. ''I'm looking for a guest—Mark Davison. It's a family emergency.''

The hotel clerk checked her computer records. ''I'm sorry, sir, but he's checked out already.''

''Was he headed back to the airport, do you know?''

''Let me get the concierge,'' the clerk said. ''He might have that information.''

The concierge picked up a moment later. ''Mr. Davison? Yes, I remember him checking out this morning. He asked for a map and directions.''

''Directions where?''

''Thunder Key.''

Chapter 14

"Hello, Leah. I'm Mark. Roman's brother-in-law. Is Roman here?"

Mark. This was the man she'd heard Roman speak to on the phone. The man who'd given Roman the psychiatrist referral. Gen's husband.

"No, he's not," she said, suddenly realizing she was just standing there, not letting him in. Rain was sheeting down. "Come inside. I'm sorry. You're getting wet."

He was soaked to the skin, a hooded slicker pressed down around his head. Gray eyes glinted from a face dripping with rain. The blustering wind whipped against dark slacks. His shoes tracked in mud as she shut the heavy door behind him. He was a tall, angular man, but his mouth was kind.

For a long beat, they stood there in the darkened hall, then he said, "I know this is strange, but I feel as if I should give you a hug. We're family, you know.''

He gave her a look that made her think he was hesitant, waiting for her permission. But the instinctive standoffishness she'd developed since her arrival in Thunder Key held her back. And something else harder to define. Cats, peas… She didn't want to hug Mark.

''It's good to see you, Leah,'' he said when she didn't move. ''It really is you. I couldn't believe it when Roman told me you were alive. I had to see for myself.''

She didn't know what to say. It was strange, as he'd said. Thoughts raced in her mind of the various things Roman had told her about her strained relationship with his family. But Mark seemed genuinely glad to see her.

''Roman's not here,'' she repeated. ''I'm sorry. He flew to New York this morning.'' How much did Mark know about the reason Roman had gone to New York? She was uncertain what to reveal. ''Would you like a drink?''

''Thanks.'' He followed her back into the bar. She set the radio on the counter, then flicked the wall switch, turning on the lights over the bar. The rest of the bar and grill lay in shadows heavier than normal at this time of the evening with the windows boarded over, black. ''We closed up because of the weather,'' she explained.

''I saw a lot of cars headed the other direction on the Overseas Highway.'' Mark threw his long legs over a bar stool. He jerked off his rain slicker. Underneath he wore a white dress shirt, no tie. The shirt was damp, and he shivered slightly in the chill of the bar. His dark brown hair looked wet, matted to his head.

''It's getting cold in here.'' Leah checked the thermostat, turned on the heater. ''So,'' she said, pivoting back, ''what would you like to drink?'' Why was he here? She didn't know what to say, what to do. She supposed eventually she would have to get used to meeting people who had known her in the past. She might never get her memory back, but people knew her even if she didn't know them. But she wished Roman was here. She didn't like meeting his family without him by her side. She didn't like not knowing what Roman had gone to New York to find out.

And she wondered if Mark knew what Roman had gone to find out. She couldn't ask him. She didn't want to hear it from Mark. However terrible it was, she needed to hear it from Roman.

She just prayed that he would still want her. The knot in her stomach that had been there all day wound tighter.

''A beer would be fine.'' Mark told her which brand he preferred. She opened a longneck bottle and slid it across the smooth counter.

The sound of rain pounded against the Shark and Fin. She could hear the hastily nailed boards creak against the windows.

''I was just going to check the radio,'' she said. ''Last I heard, the storm was still veering south, so we might be evacuating soon. Sounds like some people decided to go on and leave ahead of time.''

''Looked that way to me.'' His pale-gray eyes

scraped her as he took a long pull on the beer. "But you're still here, Leah."

"I just finished closing up the bar. The cable went out a couple hours ago—and the phones are down—but I've been listening to my battery-powered radio, checking on the storm every little bit."

"So it's just you here at the Shark and Fin."

"I sent everyone else home so they could take care of their own situations. Everyone needs to board up, get ready, in case we have to evacuate tonight."

"Why did Roman go back to New York?"

"He needed to see his parents."

Mark took another pull on his beer. "So he left you alone."

"He's coming back. Tomorrow, if he can't get back tonight. He made reservations at the Grand Palm in Miami in case I have to evacuate. He's supposed to meet me there."

"Really. Well, Roman's always on the ball, isn't he?"

Something, maybe a branch from a nearby tree, crashed outside and Leah startled. She lifted a shaky hand to push back a stray lock of hair that fell forward across her cheek. Mark's pale eyes seemed to follow her every movement.

She suddenly felt very alone in this huge, shadowy bar with this man who was her family but a stranger. Rain battered down on the building. She turned on the radio, adjusted the knob to find the station. "I was just about to go upstairs, pack a bag just in case—"

The announcer's voice came in staticky. "The hurricane has been upgraded to a category-five storm, as sustained winds increased to 160 miles per hour. Despite earlier computer models predicting the storm could head north to threaten Georgia and the Carolinas, things are now looking ominous for Florida as the storm continues to track south. Large ocean swells and dangerous surf conditions already exist up and down the Florida seaboard, and evacuations are now being ordered from the Keys to Jacksonville.''

A tingle of alarm traced along Leah's spine. She looked at Mark. He hunched over his beer, watching her as they listened to the radio report.

"As the storm continues to pick up speed, National Hurricane Center meteorologists expect it to make landfall by morning,'' the announcer continued. "If you've been waiting to head out, now's the time to stop waiting, folks.''

"That means we need to get out of here,'' Leah said. "In fact, I'm surprised you were able to get here. You must have gotten through just before the authorities closed down the highway in this direction.''

He finished his beer in one long pull. "I've been here for a few hours, Leah. I flew in to Miami this morning for a meeting. I rented a car there and drove down to Thunder Key.''

"This isn't a good time to see the Keys,'' she pointed out. "A hurricane's coming—''

"I didn't come to see the Keys.''

His gaze seemed to pin her, and she felt as if he'd touched her, even though he hadn't. She felt odd, tingly, weird. Scared, she realized. There was a hurricane on the way, of course, but there was plenty of time to evacuate. Yet her nerves tightened and she wanted to leave now. She shut off the radio.

"We need to head out.'' Her innate sense of hos-

pitality made her feel as if rushing him out was im-
polite, but he wasn't from the Keys. Maybe he didn't
understand. "The hurricane's going to hit by morning,
and it's threatening the Keys."

"How about another beer?" Mark said.

Leah blanked for a second. "We need to leave,"
she repeated. "Maybe you don't understand. In the
Keys, when they say go, you go."

"I saw everyone leave the Shark and Fin, you
know. Everyone except you, Leah. I've been watching
for hours. Waiting for you to be alone. Wondering
why Roman wasn't here. Wondering if you had your
memory back. Do you have your memory back, Leah?
Do you really have amnesia, or was that a convenient
ploy to escape your unsavory past? Couldn't face Roman once the truth was out, could you? So many questions. How about some answers? And that beer."

Leah swallowed thickly, panic swelling up inside
her. What was he talking about? He sounded nuts all
of a sudden. He'd seemed so nice and normal at the
door. *Hello, I'm Mark, your brother-in-law... Let's
hug...*

His angular face no longer looked kind. He'd been
watching the bar today. Waiting for everyone to leave.
*Couldn't face Roman once the truth was out, could
you?* What did Mark know about her past?

"I don't know what you're talking about." She had
to think. The keys were in her pocket. All she had to
do was get out the door and get into Morrie's truck.
And she had to get past the big, scary guy. No problem. "I really have amnesia. I can't remember anything before the past eighteen months."

And if he was part of her past before that, she really

didn't want to remember it now. Not while he was sitting there across the bar watching her with those pale-gray eyes that made her feel like a butterfly pinned to a posterboard.

"Look, I know Roman's family didn't much care for me—"

"I thought you didn't remember the past, Leah."

"Roman told me." Her pulse tripped hard in her veins. "I know you probably don't believe me. And that's fine. I understand." She tried to sound light. "I wouldn't believe me, either! But I don't want anything from Roman's family. Honestly. If you think I want money or something, that's not what I'm about. If Roman wants a divorce, he can have one. I'm not making any claims on him, and I would never do anything to hurt him. If there's something terrible in my past, then Roman has to decide if he can live with it. Whatever happens next is up to Roman."

Her throat almost closed up as she said those words. She was terrified that Roman *wouldn't* be able to live with it. Her *unsavory* past was how Mark had just put it. All her fears were true, then. Something awful was in her past.

"I know you're worried about Roman, but he's in New York now, and if your parents tell him whatever you apparently already know, maybe he'll never come back." She managed a casual shrug, as if she didn't care. As if her heart weren't shattering. "But right now, we need to get out of here. I'm going to go upstairs, grab some things. So, if you don't mind…"

Leave. She wanted him to leave. But if he wouldn't leave, then she would.

If he wanted to sit here at the bar with a hurricane

on the way, fine. Whatever. She didn't care. She was leaving. She wasn't even going upstairs to get her things. The keys were in her pocket. That was all she needed. That, and Roman. She hoped to God when she got to the Grand Palm, he'd be there. And that he would still want her.

She scooped her keys up from the bar counter. "I'm leaving now."

Mark reached for his slicker, pulled something dark and solid-looking out of it and pointed it straight at her chest. "I don't think so."

Thunder Key was two hours from Miami on a good day. This wasn't a good day.

Roman punched in the number to the Grand Palm as he steered the rented sedan through the blustering hell that was now the Overseas Highway. He'd picked up the cell phone with its prepaid minutes at the airport shop right after he hit ground in Miami. They'd told him his was one of the last flights in for the night. The airport was shutting down due to worsening conditions.

"Has a Leah Wells or a Leah Bradshaw checked in?" he asked for the third time since he'd left Miami.

"No, sir, she still hasn't checked in."

Roman punched the phone off and tossed it on the passenger seat, gripping the wheel again with both hands. Leah still wasn't at the Grand Palm.

And sometime today Mark had been headed for Thunder Key.

Roman had been in touch several times with his father in New York. Walter had contacted the U.S. Attorney's Office to let them know Mark was in Florida, but with a hurricane lashing its way toward shore, there wasn't much hope coordinating authorities in the state were going to move on the information tonight. Police in Miami and the Keys were consumed by emergency preparations. The only piece of luck Roman had had all afternoon was picking up a direct flight to Miami on standby within thirty minutes of arriving back at LaGuardia Airport.

Unfortunately, there wasn't a chance in hell he could connect with a flight to any of the small airports in the Keys. They were all shut down. And the drive to Thunder Key was killing him. He wanted to be there *now*. He wanted Leah in his arms *now*.

Tension speared through every nerve of his body as Roman struggled to maintain control of the car in the wind and rain. Thank God the side of the highway heading into the Keys was empty. The side heading out was packed with evacuating residents and vacationers. Roman had been stopped at a Key Largo barricade where authorities were turning around cars trying to head into the Keys.

Roman had wasted ten minutes arguing with the officer who was insisting that only emergency vehicles were being allowed to pass in this direction before he finally agreed to turn back. Then he got in his car and blew around the barriers.

He'd spent desperate hours getting back to south Florida today. No one was going to stop him from getting to Thunder Key and Leah. He only prayed he wasn't too late.

Leah stared dazedly down the barrel of Mark's gun. It was unreal. She couldn't understand what was going on. Why would Roman's brother-in-law want to shoot her? It didn't make sense.

"Look, I don't know what you're planning to do with that thing," she said carefully. "But if you really want a beer that bad, okay." She had to buy time. All she had to do was get the hell out of the bar, get to Morrie's truck, and she'd be fine.

No way was she going to consider the possibility that she wouldn't get out of this bar alive. She had a chance—a slim chance, but a chance nonetheless—of starting her life over with Roman. A chance that no matter what she'd done, he might still love her. A chance to tell him how much she loved him.

But none of that could happen if she didn't make it out of this bar tonight.

She started to reach for another beer.

"Careful," Mark warned. "Don't do anything stupid."

Slowly she opened the refrigerated case behind the bar and pulled out a beer. She popped the top with the stationary lid opener and slid the beer across the counter. Under the counter, there was a drawer of knives and assorted utensils. Heavy stainless steel mixers and other equipment. Lemon squeezers and heavy bottles of liquor. Anything would do.

Mark picked up the beer. She noticed for the first time that his hand holding the gun was slightly shaking. He looked—God, scared! *He* was scared. She didn't know if that boded well or badly for her chances of getting away from him, but she had to keep him talking till she figured it out.

"I know Roman's family doesn't like me, but this

is a little extreme, don't you think?'' She worked to keep her voice steady, calm.

He took a pull on the beer. A long one. But his eyes never left her. He set the beer down. ''This doesn't have anything to do with the Bradshaws. This is all about me and you, Leah.''

Me and you. Now he sounded scared *and* nuts.

''Okay, well, you're going to have to give me a little more information. I have amnesia, remember? So if there's something you want me to do—''

She broke off at his bark of laughter. Against the pounding storm, it echoed eerily in the empty bar.

''So you're ready to do whatever I say, are you? You weren't this accommodating eighteen months ago.'' He lowered the hand holding the gun to rest it on the bar counter, but he didn't loosen his grip on it any.

She tried to estimate how many seconds it would take her to grab one of those stainless steel mixers and chuck it at his head. Could she do it before he lifted that gun and aimed it at her heart again?

''Maybe eighteen months ago I didn't understand how serious you were,'' she said. He was real serious now.

Deadly serious.

''You made a mistake,'' Mark said.

''Definitely.'' What mistake had she made?

''You couldn't leave well enough alone.''

''I'll leave it alone now.'' No problem. Anything he wanted, she'd comply.

''Too late.''

''Why?'' She made an effort to sound simply curious while fear was making her tingle all over. She had to struggle to keep from staring at his gun. Not that his nervous, crazy eyes made her feel any better.

"You started this. It's all because of you. I thought it was over when your car went over that bridge, but it wasn't. Turns out they've been investigating me all this time. All because of you and that stupid Nikki Bates."

Leah swallowed thickly. *Nikki Bates?* Something in her mind clicked. Roman had told her Nikki Bates was the name of her maid of honor. What could her maid of honor have to do with Mark?

"Meanwhile," Mark went on angrily, "you just disappear. Nice. Screw up my life, and when yours starts to go down the toilet, you just disappear. Amnesia. How handy. But I know who you are. I know what you've done."

Leah froze, couldn't speak.

"No facing the music for you, Leah, is that it? But I have to face it. You screwed up my life, Leah."

"I didn't mean to." Oh, God, what had she done? What would ever have possessed her to mess with her raving lunatic brother-in-law?

I know who you are. I know what you've done.

Nausea rose even as cold washed down her veins.

"You should have stayed dead. But maybe this is better. Now I get to kill you twice." Mark lifted the gun again, pointed it at her. His hand shook. "I'm going down. But I'm not going alone. Don't think you can get away with this. Don't think you can ruin my life."

Nightmare reels tangled in her mind, like broken movies. *She was on a sidewalk, surrounded by soaring buildings, running, running. The man in the white coat chased her—*

Mark!

Don't think you can get away with this! Don't think you can ruin my life.

The panic attack struck full force. She was going to be sick. She couldn't think. Sweat and chills attacked her with equal force.

She couldn't breathe. She was going to choke.

"What the hell is wrong with you?" Mark's voice seemed to come from far away.

"I'm having a—" she struggled to gasp out the words "—panic attack." She threw her hand over her mouth, afraid she was going to throw up.

And somewhere in her racing mind she realized— this man who was already scared and on the edge of his rocker—was freaked out even more by her panic attack, and that this was her chance. She blinked fast a couple of times, deep breath, deep breath. She didn't think—couldn't think—just grabbed for the mixer so fast, he didn't see her.

With one adrenaline-laced lunge, she lifted and lugged the heavy stainless steel mixer over the bar, smacking him hard across the head. The gun dropped, and she heard a grunt as he stumbled backward.

She didn't wait, just grabbed the keys, almost blinded by the nausea and fear. She didn't feel her hand on the door, didn't feel the rain thudding down on her bare head, the water splashing up at her legs, didn't even hear the roar of the engine. The next thing she knew she was in Morrie's truck careening down the black, sodden road. *Breathe, breathe.* Spots flick-

ered in front of her eyes. She was going to black out
if she didn't breathe.

The vehicle skidded on the wet blacktop as she
slammed down on the brake. Panic attack plus driving—not a good combination.

Rain and wind lashed at the small truck as it skidded
to a stop. Her hand trembled on the wheel, her fingers
numbly gripping it. *Breathe, breathe.* She had to keep
driving. She had to get out of Thunder Key, before
Mark—

Lights flashed in the rearview mirror.

She spun, her gaze piercing the stormy dark. Lights.
A car was coming from the Shark and Fin!

Desperate, she slammed the truck back into gear,
the tires hydroplaning on the wet road as she accel-
erated. But Mark's rental car, newer and more powerful than Morrie's little truck, was coming faster. The
little humpbacked bridge spanning the lagoon was just
ahead, and beyond that, the Overseas Highway, and
possibly other people, maybe police or other emergency vehicles that might be out in the storm.

She pushed the truck to its limits, but the old engine
and the buffeting wind made it impossible to go any
faster. Terror choked her throat as the lights grew
brighter, closer, in the rearview mirror.

Another stormy night, another bridge, exploded in
her mind. *He was going to drive her off the road. He
was going to kill her—again!*

She felt as if her head was being torn apart.
Thoughts, images, crashed against one another. New
York City. Mark's office. Nikki's apartment. Bottles
and bottles of prescribed pills. Far more pills than
Nikki needed, in far higher doses and dangerous com-

binations. Leah had done the research, had taken the pills to her own doctor and then to the police. She'd started asking questions. And Mark had found out.

I know who you are. I know what you've done. Stop talking to the police! I'll tell Roman everything about your past. Divorce him and he'll never know.

Dizzy shock spun through Leah. He was talking about her foster father, she knew that suddenly, sharply. The one who'd thrown her against the refrigerator door for wearing makeup. Blood everywhere, screams. But she didn't do it. She didn't kill her foster father. Her mind reeled with desperate snatches of memory that wouldn't come together.

Do you want to ruin Roman's life? Mark had the divorce papers all ready. Roman's father had had his lawyer draw them up. All she had to do was take them to Roman.

But she didn't want to do it. She wasn't ready to give up on her marriage. And she couldn't stop talking to the police about Nikki. She remembered Roman! And she loved him. God, she loved him. But she didn't want to ruin his life.

The car swerved up alongside her as she reached the bridge, slamming into the driver's side door. There were new lights up ahead, coming toward them from the Overseas Highway! She struggled to keep the small truck on the road as Mark's car struck her again. The wheel spun in her hands as the truck flew through the guardrail. The lagoon crashed up to meet her scream.

Roman's car swooped down the tiny road leading to the Shark and Fin, battling the wind and rain as he

raced straight toward the bridge, almost running head-
first into a car careening over the bridge. Skidding
sideways, he barely avoided a collision as a wind-
lashed tree smacked down in the middle of the road,
striking the other car's windshield with thunderous
force.

Leah. Oh, God, was that Leah?

He hit the brakes, slipped into a dangerous spin,
stopping short of the bridge just as a figure staggered
out from the car.

Reaching instinctively for the cell phone, Roman
punched in the emergency number even as he burst
out of the car. Rain gushed around him. He was
drenched instantly. He couldn't hear the operator's response over the storm, but he clipped out the information and prayed for a miracle. The figure lurched
out of the thick storm, close enough now to identify.
Fear, heavier than rain, washed down.

"Mark?" A gust whipped the word away.

Blood and rain poured down his brother-in-law's
face. He looked dazed, stumbling in the fierce wind.
Roman realized Mark wasn't even looking at him. He
hadn't heard him, and he was focused completely on
the other side of the road. On the lagoon. Roman pivoted, seeing only then.

Morrie's truck. Leah.

Anguished fury took him. Cell phone still gripped
in his fist, he raced across the road. Not again. This
couldn't be happening again. He'd lost Leah once this
way—he couldn't lose her again. This time had to be
different. This time he was here.

He charged for Mark, knocking him to the ground
with one hard blow, then Roman went on, fighting the

gale-force winds. He left Mark behind him on the road. Roman didn't care how badly he was hurt, didn't stop. If Mark had driven Leah off the road—again— he'd come back and kill him.

But first he had to find Leah. Had to hold her in his arms. Had to tell her he loved her.

Sliding feetfirst down the culvert alongside the bridge, into the dark lagoon, he could see the truck sticking crazily nose down in the shallow water and mud. Please, God, let her be alive. Heart in his throat, he dropped the phone by the marshy shore.

The lagoon felt like syrup as he pushed his feet toward the truck, his gaze piercing desperately into the crashed cab. Wind and rain ripped at his vision, but as he reached the driver's side door, he saw her.

Dark, tangled wet hair, blood. Still. So still.

Roman felt part of himself die even as panicked anger drove him on. He couldn't even feel his fingers, cold and numb, as he struggled to get the door open in the hurricane's fury.

"Leah!"

And she lifted her head.

His heart damn near exploded in his chest.

"Roman." Her voice was torn away by the storm, but it didn't matter.

Gently he cupped his hands on her face. Through the cold and wet, she was warm. She was alive. And he had an irrational sense of complete peace in the midst of the rioting storm. But he had to get her out of there.

He pulled back to examine her.

She was bleeding from a nasty-looking cut over one eye, and he could see she was in pain. "Are you all right?'' He shouted the words over the wind and rain. She nodded, and he started to pull her out of the cab, into his arms, but she resisted.

''He's got a gun! Mark's got a gun!''

Dear God. In all the years Mark had been married to Gen, Roman had never known his brother-in-law to own a gun. Roman tore away from Leah, ready to do whatever he had to in order to protect her. The joy of finding Leah whole and alive transformed to shattering dread.

Through the near-blinding rain, he saw Mark stumbling down the culvert, toward the lagoon. Even across the distance, his eyes adjusted to the stormy dark now, he could see Mark's flat, dead-looking eyes. Blood came out of his mouth and nose. Roman was no doctor, but he knew Mark had to have been badly injured when the tree crashed down on his car.

''Mark, you're hurt, don't make this worse,'' Roman shouted, blocking Leah from the gun now waving in Mark's hand.

''It can't get worse!'' Mark kept coming, staggering into the lagoon. ''She ruined my life. It's all her fault. She went to the police.'' He continued lurching toward them. ''She's a murdering bitch,'' he spat thickly, ''and she went to the police about me? I was only trying to help people!''

''You were helping yourself,'' Roman shouted. ''Illegal drugs. Health care fraud. Kickbacks. Leah didn't do that to you. You did it to yourself.''

His gaze pinned Mark even as Roman's mind tore desperately for a way out, even if all he could do was keep him talking till he got the chance to overpower

him or he passed out. But what he feared was he'd
shoot the gun before that happened.

Mark wobbled where he stood, dropped to his knees
in the dark muddy water, his face paling under the
sluicing blood. Still he waved the gun drunkenly.

"She's a murdering, lying bitch!" Mark's voice
was weaker, slurring. "Get out of the way, Roman. If
I have to shoot you to get to her, I will. I'm not going
down alone. She's going down with me."

"You're ruined Mark," Roman ground out.
"Shooting either one of us won't change that. You'll
just make it worse—for yourself, for Gen. You love
Gen, Mark. I know you do. Don't make this worse for
her by doing something crazy now."

"I can't do anything for Gen!" Mark slurred out,
lurching to his feet again with the gun. "It's over.
They know everything. There's nothing I can do." He
stood there, wobbling.

"Yes, there is," Roman urged him. Could he overpower him? Mark was pale in the stormy dark, blood
oozing from his ears now. It was worth the risk. He
would do anything to protect Leah. "You can *not*
make it worse, Mark. No matter what it takes, I'm not
going to let you hurt Leah again."

He eyed Mark, waiting for the right second to
pounce. The gun shook in Mark's hand, and he
seemed barely able to focus.

"Don't do this to Gen," he tried one last time.

Then Roman felt Leah shove past him, out of the
cab. "It's me he wants."

Mark swayed in reaction, and terror washed Roman's mind in the split instant the gun went off.

Chapter 15

Leah felt numb, listless, as the medical technician finished stitching the cut above her eye. Inside a historic church in Orchid Key, a staging ground for emergency personnel still in the islands, the sound of the lashing storm outside played on.

It was finally over. The aftermath had seemed neverending. Roman's desperate 911 call had been patched through to emergency personnel nearest Thunder Key. But they'd arrived too late to change the outcome.

Mark was dead, by his own hand. The nightmare was only beginning for Roman's family. Even in the midst of a hurricane, national news crews—on hand for the weather crisis—felt as if they'd bagged two birds with one stone when they caught on to the drama of a wealthy doctor on the run from federal authorities. From illegal drugs and health fraud to attempted murder and suicide, the story had everything the voracious twenty-four-hour cable news world fed on.

"You're going to be just fine," the technician said. "The cut goes right through the eyebrow line. The scar won't even show."

As if she cared about a scar. The nightmare was just beginning for her, as well.

You're going to be just fine. Was she? Roman had talked to his parents and must have learned the shameful past she'd wanted to protect him from, learned that she'd lied about the kind of person she truly was. There were no more secrets between her and Roman. Except one—that she had regained her memory in the trauma of being forced off the bridge by Mark. All the pieces had fallen into horrible, heartbreaking place.

Roman had been devastated by Mark's suicide, and in the shocking moments when he'd done everything he could to save his brother-in-law before police and emergency medics had arrived, there had been no time to talk.

She didn't even know where Roman was now. They'd been separated in the stormy chaos while the police took Roman's statement on the scene and medics diagnosed the chest pain she was experiencing as due to multiple rib fractures. She'd been on the verge of blacking out when they'd put her in the ambulance.

In the sanctuary of the solid rock church, families with sleeping bags and bottles of water and crying babies surrounded her. At nearly midnight, the hurricane was pounding its way toward them at a relentless speed. A direct hit on the Keys wasn't expected, but it would be a long night nevertheless.

"They've closed all the bridges now," the techni-

cian told Leah. "The wind and surf conditions are too
dangerous. You'll have to shelter here tonight."

They'd had to cut off Leah's shirt to wrap her ribs
in an immobilizing swathe that kept her left arm
strapped to her chest. One of the technicians had dug
up a spare emergency medic's shirt that buttoned
down the front, draping it over her left shoulder since
she could only move her right arm.

Helped by the technician, Leah slid carefully off the
table the medics had brought in for their makeshift
emergency area.

"If you'll go out of the sanctuary and to the right,
follow that corridor and there's a fellowship hall," the
technician told her. "They should have some extra
blankets, pillows and some food and water there."

Leah wasn't hungry, but she made her slow, painful
way down the hall. There were several media vans
with correspondents giving live reports in the fierce
winds outside the church, but inside, the reporters
were interviewing evacuees. If they knew who she
was, they'd want to talk to her about Mark. And she
didn't want to talk to them. Thank God the medics
had protected her privacy. For all the reporters knew,
she was just another victim of the storm.

Her heart tripped in her already-painful chest as she
entered the fellowship hall. Her gaze darted, hoping,
praying… But she didn't see Roman in the crowded
hall.

How would he feel about her now? Whether she
had wanted it to end this way or not, her persistence
after Nikki's death had apparently resulted in a full-
scale investigation of Mark Davison's practice. She
was still overwhelmed by what had transpired in the

past eighteen months. She felt like Rip van Winkle, awaking years later instead of only eighteen months, and lost in her new world.

She'd never guessed her suspicions and questions about all the pain pills she'd found in Nikki's apartment would have had such far-reaching consequences. She ached for her friend who shouldn't have died. And she ached for Roman and his family for their loss, as well.

And most of all, she just ached. Her heart was torn apart. She remembered their marriage, every last detail. Their whirlwind courtship and the struggles of meshing their very different lifestyles. He thought he'd been a bastard to her, but she was the one who'd kept so many secrets from him. She'd never given him a chance. Would he give her a chance now? Could Roman ever forgive her for her role in his sister's devastation? On top of that, could he forgive her for the secrets of her past she'd kept from him during their marriage?

She didn't know how to find him, and worse, she didn't know if he wanted to find her. The night stretched ahead interminably.

The church fellowship center was crowded with families. Children sat on metal folding chairs at long tables, eating cookies and clasping teddy bears, or curled up in corners with pillows and books or electronic handheld games, their parents by turns talking or fitfully dozing. Emergency relief workers handed out food and drinks and blankets from the church kitchen. The atmosphere was part lock-in sleepover party, part funeral wake. She was surrounded by strangers, and completely alone.

As she walked through the packed hall, she passed a reporter giving a live report.

"Davison fled to Miami after federal authorities moved in on his Manhattan clinic. At least ten deaths have been linked to illegal narcotics distributed through the clinic. The doctor faced life in prison and millions in fines before going on a shooting rampage in the Keys, only adding to the chaos authorities are dealing with here as the hurricane closes in."

Shooting rampage? Leah kept going, wanting to get as far away as possible from the correspondent and the sensational reporting that could only hurt Roman and his family more.

Then the heavy door to the outside banged open.

Roman stood there in the Orchid Key church building, soaked, exhausted, desperate. Then he found her.

He couldn't swallow, couldn't move, for the longest pulse beat of his life. If there were a hundred strangers in the hall, he didn't notice them. Only her. Roman went straight toward her. She looked tired and hurting and like hell, but beautiful just the same.

A media correspondent started toward him, followed by a cameraman hefting heavy equipment. He'd already dealt with the groups of reporters outside, and he was in no mood for more. Unfortunately, as a Bradshaw, his family appeared on the pages of the national newspapers enough for his face to be instantly recognizable to the cable press.

"I have no comment." He followed up with a hard glare, and the reporter backed away.

Roman reached Leah.

"I thought I'd lost you," he said. "I looked around

and you were gone.'' She was wearing a medic's shirt, and he could see one of her arms was strapped to her chest. Dammit. Why hadn't he known she was hurt?

"My ribs were fractured in the crash. I didn't realize that was why I was in pain. They put me in the ambulance so quickly, I didn't have a chance to find you.'' Her voice sounded timid.

"Are you all right?'' He reached out for her, then dropped his hands, not sure how to touch her. Not sure she wanted him to touch her.

"I'm fine,'' she said, and her voice came out thick.

She was trying to be strong again. Trying not to cry.

"This is my fault,'' he said. "I should never have left you in Thunder Key this morning. I should never have—''

"Roman, no,'' she whispered. "You couldn't have known. You thought I was safe. I thought I was safe.''

"He hurt you.'' He sounded—and felt—devastated. "I'm the one who told him you were alive. And he could have killed you…''

"But he didn't.'' She reached out now, touched him with her free hand. Her fingertips grazed his face. "And you didn't know. Couldn't have known. I'm so sorry. About Mark. And Gen.''

He took hold of her hand, squeezed it in his. "It's going to be painful for her, and for my parents,'' he said roughly. "But nobody's blaming you. Not anymore. I just got off the phone with my dad. He called the cell when I was on the way here in the police cruiser. The feds were there at the apartment again this afternoon. There's no doubt in anyone's mind now that Mark knew what he was doing. It's hitting my family pretty hard. I think they're pretty much going through what I went through eighteen months ago when I lost you. Realizing that the things they thought were important really aren't. Money and power... It just doesn't matter when you're facing life and death. God, Leah, I was so afraid when I looked around and you were gone.''

A dark anguish crossed Leah's face.

"You know I'm responsible for the investigation into Mark's practice,'' she said. "If I hadn't pushed so hard after Nikki's death—'' She stopped, swallowed, pulled her hand away from his. She was distancing herself, and it was killing him. "And that's not all. You must know about my past now.''

He started to speak, but she cut him off. "I remember everything now, Roman. Just before the crash—it all came back. I haven't even had a chance to sort it all out. I feel—'' she shook her head "—out of place, you know? I don't know how to explain. It's like I woke up on a different planet, and yet it's the same. I'm the same person, but a stranger.''

What the hell did this mean? He was terrified suddenly.

"Leah.'' He reached for her again.

"No,'' she whispered brokenly. "I just want you to know that I didn't want to divorce you. Not ever. I didn't have those papers drawn up. I would never have given up on our marriage. Mark brought those papers to me and told me what your parents had found out about my past. He told me I was going to ruin your life. He wanted me to stop talking to the police about Nikki and when I refused, he became angry, and I was scared. You were working late that night and I'd come to the building to find you, but Mark was there. He'd followed me, and he was angry, making threats. I couldn't get past him into the building. So I ran back to the car. And then I started driving. I just kept going, and I got lost. I have no idea how I ended up on that road that night. I wasn't running away from you. I wasn't leaving you. I was just trying to lose Mark, and the next thing I knew, he was ramming my car. He pushed me over the bridge. And then—'' She stopped.

And then the nightmare had begun, for both of them.

Roman's heart filled painfully. "Leah—"

"You have to know that I lied to you,'' she went on, not giving him a chance to speak. She seemed determined to get it all out, now, at once. "I was never the woman you thought I was.''

"You're more than I thought you were.''

"No. I lied. I hid my past.''

"Your foster father.''

"I didn't kill him.'' Her voice trembled, and she took another deep breath. "It wasn't only me he abused. He abused my foster mother, too. And I wouldn't testify against her. They put me in a juvenile home. I had a bad history—I'd been through a lot of homes. I lost my parents when I was five, and for a long time I wouldn't even speak. Foster parents didn't know what to do with me, and I acted out. I can't blame them. I went through so many homes, and then I ended up with the Hendersons.''

She stopped, swallowed hard, looked away from him as if ashamed to meet his eyes. Then slowly, painfully, she looked at him from heart-torn eyes. "I knew she was going to do it. I knew. And I could have told somebody, or done something. I don't know. But I hated him," she said thickly.

"And when the police came, I lied for her. I told them someone had broken in. They didn't believe me or her. But they could never prove it. I think they really didn't know which one of us had done it. They sent me to the detention center till I was of age and could go out on my own. I went to New York and pretended I was someone else. Someone carefree and happy, without a past. When your family found out—"

"You were seventeen, Leah." He wanted to wrap his arms around her so much his whole body ached, but he was so afraid of hurting her. "And I never doubted you weren't a murderer. I knew it wasn't in you. As for knowing what your foster mother would do... How *could* you have stopped it? You'd both been hurt by him too many times..."

"I had no right to marry someone like you," she went. "Your family was right."

"They were wrong!"

"I should have told you the truth. I should have trusted you. And I don't know how you can ever trust me." Tears filled her eyes, spilled over.

"How could you have trusted me? I didn't trust myself," he said, cupping her face, still so afraid of hurting her tender ribs. Her shining eyes ripped him apart. "I didn't trust the way you made me feel. You were everything I ever wanted and didn't know I wanted. You made me feel things I'd never known before."

"You thought I was perfect," she cried softly. "And I was so far from it."

"No," he argued, almost angry now—at himself, not her—that she had held so much inside when they were married. And he had let her because of his own fears. "I thought you were perfect for *me*. And that scared me to death. I didn't know you could love someone that much, and I was sure I'd lose you. I worked too hard and ignored you, and I was such a bastard, I made sure I *would* lose you."

He skimmed his touch down her face, tracing her tears.

"I love you," he whispered roughly. "And I need you. When I thought I'd lost you, it was as if my world went dark. It was a miracle that I found you again. Ever since I came to Thunder Key and saw you that first day in the bar, I knew this was where I was supposed to be. Here. With you. I dream of our life here, the kind of man I would be. I dream of our grandkids building sand castles on the beach in thirty years. I really like that dream."

She made a soft sound in her throat, a half sob, half laugh. "I like that dream, too."

Hope rose inside him, but he had to be sure she really knew what she was getting into. He was a changed man, but he was still a Bradshaw, and old habits would die hard.

"I'm not ever going to be an easy man to live with," he said. "I'm still the same driven bastard I ever was, and I'll have my moments when I lose sight of what's important. I'll buy the Shark and Fin, and one day I'll wake up and think I have to turn it into a restaurant chain across Florida. And you'll have to just pull me back into bed and make love to me till I beg for mercy."

Now she did laugh.

"Oh, that hurt." She reached up to touch her chest. "I can't laugh."

"I want you to laugh every day," he said. "I want to laugh with you. And if you cry, I'll cry with you. I don't want you to be afraid of anything with me."

"Only if you promise not to be afraid of anything with me."

"Well, I'm dying right now," he admitted, "because I want to hold you so bad, but I'm afraid if I take you into my arms, I'll hurt you."

"Please take me in your arms. And don't let go. Ever. I love you."

Her face was bright and her eyes glowed, and he saw again the Leah he remembered. Free and happy and full of hope. He'd made her whole, too. He drew her gently into his arms, bent his head to kiss her lips as she tipped her face to meet him, and he knew there would be no more nightmares.

Only the sweetest dreams.

Epilogue

The Miami hospital was silent at midnight.

Roman peeked into Room 502. Leah looked up from the bed in the moon-striped dark of the room. At her breast, an infant with a fuzz of dark hair suckled. And Leah smiled her fantastic smile.

"Hey, there," Roman said softly, coming into the room, quiet but for the steady sound of the nursing babe at his wife's swollen breast.

"She's all cleaned up now," Leah told him. "They said they'd let me sleep, but I'd rather be with her. And you. But you're tired, aren't you? It's okay if you want to go back to Thunder Key, get some sleep—"

"Not a chance." Roman wasn't going anywhere. He sat on the edge of the bed, watching his beautiful wife and their two-hour-old baby girl. It had been a long ten months since the night they'd sheltered at the Orchid Key church. The bar had been damaged by the hurricane-force winds. They'd moved into one of the little shotgun houses in Thunder Key, which was just fine since they needed a nursery now.

They'd already rebuilt the Shark and Fin, just as they'd rebuilt their interrupted marriage.

"I just got off the phone with my parents," he told her. "They've been calling the hospital all night."

"How are they?" Leah's face tensed.

All these months later, it still hurt her when she thought of her role in his family's tragedy, Roman knew. Leah felt others' pain as keenly as she felt her own. And even though his family ultimately hadn't blamed her after Mark's death, she still regretted that it had happened and that she'd played any part in it.

Not that his parents had completely accepted her, but they had accepted that what Mark had done was his own fault. And they'd accepted that Leah was going to be Roman's wife forever. Roman had made it clear they didn't have a choice about that. And maybe, just maybe, this new Bradshaw who had just come into the world tonight would make a difference.

His mother had sounded like herself again on the phone. By noon tomorrow, Roman suspected every shop on Madison Avenue would be cleaned out. His mother couldn't wait to shop for baby clothes.

"I think we're going to be getting a lot of boxes from New York," he told Leah. "And as for my dad—he said to tell you we'd better not stop yet. He wants a lot of grandchildren."

"He's hoping one of them will want to go into the business."

Roman shrugged. "It'll be up to them." He leaned down to kiss his wife. "They're going to have a different childhood than either you or I had. They're going to grow up on Thunder Key. And they'll choose their own futures.''

He'd chosen his. With Leah. And it was sweeter than it had ever been before. Over the months, Leah had come out of her shell. She was the old Leah again—happy and fun and amazing, but thank God he wasn't the old Roman. He was happy, too.

''Did you invite them to come see the baby?'' Leah asked.

Roman nodded. They'd been to New York, once. It had been a difficult trip. But slowly his family was piecing their lives back together, and getting to know their daughter-in-law—finally—was part of that process. They'd seen how happy Roman was with her, and it had been a start.

''They're going to come visit in a few weeks,'' he said.

''What about Gen? How is she?''

Roman touched the soft hair on his baby's head. She was asleep, milk drooling out of the corner of her little baby lips. Leah adjusted her gown, covering the bared nipple.

''She's going to be all right,'' Roman said. ''She's been living with my parents since the baby was born.'' Gen had been only a few weeks pregnant when Mark had died. Neither she nor Mark had even known a child was on the way. ''The baby's doing fine, growing. She says she's not going back to work at the firm. She's thinking about moving out to the country somewhere, building a house and raising horses.''

''Horses?'' Leah lifted her brows.

''Yeah. Who knew? Gen says she always loved

horses, but Dad wanted her to go into the business. But she doesn't care about any of that now.''

"Good for Gen." Leah smiled, then added, "Your poor dad."

"He's got lots of nieces and nephews who are probably falling all over themselves with joy at their luck that Gen and I have left the firm, giving them the chance to head to the top," Roman said, then leaned in to kiss his wife again. "But what do they know?" he whispered against her sweet lips. He loved his wife, loved his baby, loved his life. "We're the lucky ones."

* * * * *

I N T I M A T E   M O M E N T S™

This November, Silhouette Intimate Moments presents the thrilling finale of the continuity

 No one is alone...

IN DESTINY'S SHADOW

by award-winning author

Ingrid Weaver

Loner Anthony Caldwell spent months searching for the evil criminal mastermind who threatened his family. When he met beautiful investigative reporter Melina Becker, he knew she could lead him straight to his nemesis—but he didn't count on the curious reporter breaking down the barriers to his heart and soul. For the first time in his life, Anthony gave his trust to another and told Melina the secrets of his past...and shared a passion he'd never thought possible. But when danger caught up to them, Anthony knew he would have to face his destiny to save the woman of his dreams.

Don't miss this powerful story—only from Silhouette Books

Available at your favorite retail outlet

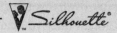

If you enjoyed what you just read,
then we've got an offer you can't resist!

Take 2 bestselling love stories FREE!

Plus get a FREE surprise gift!

Clip this page and mail it to Silhouette Reader Service™

IN U.S.A.	IN CANADA
3010 Walden Ave.	P.O. Box 609
P.O. Box 1867	Fort Erie, Ontario
Buffalo, N.Y. 14240-1867	L2A 5X3

YES! Please send me 2 free Silhouette Intimate Moments® novels and my free surprise gift. After receiving them, if I don't wish to receive anymore, I can return the shipping statement marked cancel. If I don't cancel, I will receive 6 brand-new novels every month, before they're available in stores! In the U.S.A., bill me at the bargain price of $4.24 plus 25¢ shipping and handling per book and applicable sales tax, if any*. In Canada, bill me at the bargain price of $4.99 plus 25¢ shipping and handling per book and applicable taxes**. That's the complete price and a savings of at least 10% off the cover prices—what a great deal! I understand that accepting the 2 free books and gift places me under no obligation ever to buy any books. I can always return a shipment and cancel at any time. Even if I never buy another book from Silhouette, the 2 free books and gift are mine to keep forever.

245 SDN DZ9A
345 SDN DZ9C

Name	(PLEASE PRINT)	
Address	Apt.#	
City	State/Prov.	Zip/Postal Code

Not valid to current Silhouette Intimate Moments® subscribers.

Want to try two free books from another series?
Call 1-800-873-8635 or visit www.morefreebooks.com.

* Terms and prices subject to change without notice. Sales tax applicable in N.Y.
** Canadian residents will be charged applicable provincial taxes and GST.
All orders subject to approval. Offer limited to one per household].
® are registered trademarks owned and used by the trademark owner and or its licensee.

INMOM04R   ©2004 Harlequin Enterprises Limited

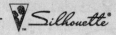

SPECIAL EDITION™

Coming in November to
Silhouette Special Edition
The fifth book in the exciting continuity

DARK SECRETS. OLD LIES. NEW LOVES.

THE MARRIAGE ACT

(Silhouette Special Edition #1646)

by

Elissa Ambrose

Plain-Jane accountant Linda Mailer had never done
anything shocking in her life—until she had a one-night
stand with a sexy detective and found herself pregnant!
Then she discovered that her anonymous Romeo was
none other than Tyler Carlton, the man spearheading the
investigation of her beleaguered boss, Walter Parks. Tyler
wanted to give his child a real family, and convinced
Linda to marry him. Their passion sparked in close
quarters, but Linda was wary of Tyler's motives and afraid
of losing her heart. Was he using her to get to Walter—or
had they found the true love they'd both longed for?

Available at your favorite retail outlet.

Silhouette Desire

Coming in November 2004 from

Silhouette Desire

Author Peggy Moreland presents

Sins of a Tanner

Melissa Jacobs dreaded asking her ex-lover Whit Tanner
for help, but when the smashingly sexy rancher came
to her aid, hours spent at her home turned into
hours of intimacy. Yet Melissa was hiding a sinful
secret that could either tear them apart,
or bring them together forever.

The TANNERS of TEXAS

**Born to a legacy of scandal—
destined for love as deep as their Texas roots!**

Available at your favorite retail outlet.

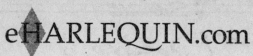

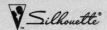

INTIMATE MOMENTS™

Presenting a new book

by popular author

LYN STONE

Part of her exciting miniseries

Dangerous.

Deadly.

Desirable.

Under the Gun

(Silhouette Intimate Moments #1330)

After escaping the bullet that killed his twin, Special Agent
Will Griffin awakens from a coma to discover the killer at his
bedside. Thanks to some quick action, he's on the run again.
But this time it's with the one woman—Special Ops Agent
Holly Amberson—whose very proximity makes him feel like
he's under the gun. Because once the assassin
is caught, Will knows his life won't mean
a damn without Holly in it.

Available in November 2004 at your favourite retail outlet

Be sure to look for these earlier titles in the Special Ops miniseries:
Down to the Wire (Silhouette Intimate Moments #1281)
Against the Wall (Silhouette Intimate Moments #1295)

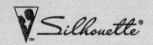

COMING NEXT MONTH